Praise for the *New York [Times]*

THE
GIRL OF F[IRE]
AND
THORNS
TRILOGY

"Intense, unique. . . . Definitely recommended."
—Veronica Roth, author of the nationally best-selling *Divergent*

"Elisa is a wonderful, believable hero,
the kind that every reader can imagine as herself. Engrossing."
—Tamora Pierce, author of the *New York Times* best-seller *Bloodhound*

"I love this series to pieces, and so should you."
—Marie Lu, *New York Times* best-selling author of *Legend*

"One of the most brilliant modern YA fantasies on the market today.
This is YA fantasy as it should be."
—Beth Revis, author of the nationally best-selling *Across the Universe*

"With *The Girl of Fire and Thorns*, Carson joins the ranks of writers
like Kristin Cashore, Megan Whalen Turner, and Tamora Pierce
as one of YA's best writers of high fantasy."—*Locus Magazine*

"Rae Carson has proved she's a master
and has shaken up the YA genre."—USAToday.com

"There are books you like, and books you love,
and then there are the ones that make you go past
'love' and straight into, 'I think I may need to marry this book.'"
—Rachel Hawkins, author of the *New York Times* best-selling *Hex Hall*

"Rae Carson's heroine is a perfect blend of the ordinary
and the extraordinary. I loved her."
—Megan Whalen Turner, author of the Newbery Honor book *The Thief*

CALGARY PUBLIC LIBRARY

NOV - - 2014

FIRE

THE GIRL OF FIRE AND THORNS STORIES

THE SHADOW CATS
THE SHATTERED MOUNTAIN
THE KING'S GUARD

RAE CARSON

GREENWILLOW BOOKS
An Imprint of HarperCollins *Publishers*

This book is a work of fiction. References to real people, events, establishments, organizations, or locales are intended only to provide a sense of authenticity, and are used to advance the fictional narrative. All other characters, and all incidents and dialogue, are drawn from the author's imagination and are not to be construed as real.

The Girl of Fire and Thorns Stories
Text copyright © 2012, 2013 by Rae Carson
The Shadow Cats was first published as a Greenwillow original ebook in 2012; *The Shattered Mountain* and *The King's Guard* were first published as Greenwillow original ebooks in 2013.

All rights reserved. No part of this book may be used or reproduced in any manner whatsoever without written permission except in the case of brief quotations embodied in critical articles and reviews. Printed in the United States of America. For information address HarperCollins Children's Books, a division of HarperCollins Publishers, 195 Broadway, New York, NY 10007.

www.epicreads.com
The text of this book is set in 11-point Bell.
Book design by Paul Zakris

Library of Congress Cataloging-in-Publication Data
Carson, Rae.
The Girl of fire and thorns stories / Rae Carson.
pages cm
"Greenwillow Books."
Originally published as digital-only.
Summary: Three novellas tell of Elisa, as Alodia discovers her sister's true potential as the bearer, friend Mara tells how she came to be in the rebel camp where Elisa is taken by her kidnappers, and guard commander and true love, Hector, discovers a secret he must keep forever.
ISBN 978-0-06-233433-6 (paperback)
[1. Kings, queens, rulers, etc.—Fiction. 2. Prophesies—Fiction. 3. Magic—Fiction. 4. Sisters—Fiction. 5. Friendship—Fiction. 6. Love—Fiction.] I. Title.
PZ7.C2423Gj 2014
[Fic]—dc23   2014019512

14 15 16 17 18 LP/RRDH 10 9 8 7 6 5 4 3 2 1
First Edition

GREENWILLOW BOOKS

FOR ELLEN KEY HARRIS-BRAUN,
WHOSE WORKSHOP CHANGED MY LIFE

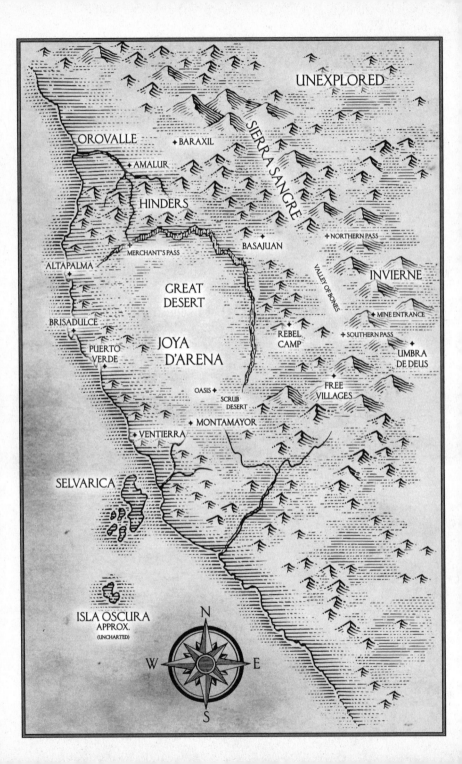

TABLE OF CONTENTS

A Note from Rae Carson

When I was an aspiring author, a common bit of advice I heard from my mentors was that I ought to imagine a rich and unique personal history for every single character, even the minor ones. This history wouldn't necessarily make it onto the page, they told me, but it would inform every gesture, every bit of dialogue, every interaction, making the characters come to life in visceral ways.

I took this advice to heart. In fact, I probably went a little overboard imagining the tiniest details of my secondary characters' lives *before* they were immortalized in the world of *The Girl of Fire and Thorns* and became part of Elisa's journey.

But only the *outcomes* of these histories made it into the pages of the trilogy. For instance, the reader watches Princess Alodia yearn for her sister even while marrying her off and sending her far away—but doesn't know why.

The reader sees that Lady Mara bears terrible scars, both on her skin and in her heart—but doesn't know why.

The reader recognizes that Lord Hector carries the weight of secrets, that he has been given extraordinary responsibilities far beyond his years—but doesn't know why.

This collection, published after the trilogy is complete, finally reveals *why*. Each story shows a pivotal moment in the life of one of my favorite characters from *The Girl of Fire and Thorns.* They are histories I imagined years ago, and I'm delighted that I finally have an opportunity to share them. I hope they help you get to know and love Alodia, Mara, and Hector the way I do.

THE SHADOW CATS

I crouch hidden among the boulders, my body broken and bloodied. Below me, someone is about to murder my best friend, the one person who understands me.

If I act, I will likely lose my own life. If I don't, I'll lose so much more.

A chorus of aches and injuries scream at me to stop, but I creep forward. My fingers close on a rock, the only weapon at hand.

I despise open carriages, even in the finest weather or upon the smoothest road, and this journey offers neither. The air in the mountains is brisk with cold, as though spring is reluctant to visit here. The mule path we follow shows little evidence of human care; it's ragged with rocks and roots and steep switchbacks. My rear aches from the constant jolting. It's a wonder we haven't lost a carriage wheel yet.

But during the last few days, we've passed through remote villages that no representative of the royal family has visited in more than a decade. And I find myself grateful for the one advantage an open carriage provides: it allows me to observe.

What I see fills me with dread.

People line the road as we pass. They are crusted with dirt and weathered by sun and wind, wearing clothes so ragged I would not dress my scullery maids in them. They clutch their children to their chests and watch our procession with curiosity, maybe a touch of misgiving. But as my carriage approaches, the heralds call out, "Her Royal Highness Juana-

Alodia de Riqueza, Crown Princess of Orovalle!" And the curiosity I read in their faces turns to outright hostility.

Some kneel and bow their heads in proper supplication. But others stand stubbornly until my guards rest their hands meaningfully on their scabbards and bark the order to show respect.

I hold my head high and school my features into bland pleasantness. It's the expression Lord Zito, my personal steward, says often causes him trouble, because he knows it means I'm hiding something.

And right now, what I don't want the world to see is how angry I am with my father, the king. The situation is even worse than I feared. Papá has neglected this district dreadfully since the end of the last war with Invierne. Now the wealthiest here ignore the capital, preferring to trade with Joya d'Arena, the kingdom across the border, while the poorest flee into the jungle-choked Hinders to join the Perditos, bandits who steal whatever they can from whoever they find. It's the perfect recipe for rebellion.

When I am queen, I will put a stop to it all. I will regain the loyalty and trust of our people. I will make this region strong again. And to do it, I will need the help of Paxón, the conde who rules this region.

Which is why, when we received an invitation to the wedding of Conde Paxón and a certain Lady Calla, I *insisted* to Papá that I be allowed to attend. Furthermore, I insisted on bringing wedding gifts fit for a royal ally—with well-armed soldiers to deliver them.

According to my informants, his bride-to-be is a lovely young woman with a wealthy father. But it would not matter to me if she were a crofter's daughter. It's past time for the conde to marry. He was a tremendous soldier in the last war. Afterward, he pursued hunting and drinking with the same ruthless tenacity—until he met his match in a giant boar who gored him. If it were up to me, I would knight the boar for putting an end to Paxón's wild ways and making him look to his legacy. A conde with a family is a man with something to lose, and a man with something to lose is always more eager to stand behind the shield of a strong king. Or queen.

I intend to know his measure and show him mine before he becomes my vassal.

A ruckus from behind causes me to whirl in my seat, and my temper flares. My fifteen-year-old sister, Elisa, follows me in her own carriage, accompanied by her nurse, Lady Ximena. She always carries a bag full of pastries when she travels, and now she throws bits of bread to the scrawny children lining our rocky road.

Mothers urge them toward the carriage, knowing the guards will be reluctant to draw blades against them. Emboldened, the children slip through their formation and bang on the sides of the carriage, thrusting up dirty hands for more. A baguette drops onto the dusty earth. Three small boys scramble for it, pulling it to shreds.

My sister is delighted. She grins enormously and breaks her bread into pieces as fast as she can. I signal to Zito, but he already moves toward her carriage, barking orders. That's the exact moment Elisa realizes her predicament, that her naive generosity has created a mob. The smile dies on her face as she recoils against her nurse.

My hand flies to my bodice where my dagger lies hidden. The guards shout at everyone to disperse, but one boy tries to climb inside the carriage. Lady Ximena shoves him back into the waiting arms of a guard. A woman shrieks—the boy's mother?—as, finally, the guards draw their swords.

And just like that, the children slink away. Most melt into the leafless trees, until only a few remain to observe our procession from a cautious distance.

The horses pulling Elisa's carriage swish their tails and toss their heads nervously, which makes it difficult for me to discern if she's all right. I crane my neck, rising up from my seat.

Our eyes meet. She gazes at me sullenly, as if daring me to scold. Slowly, deliberately, I turn away from her and settle back onto my bench.

She's wrong—I don't want to scold her. Now that I know she's unharmed, I want to smack her. Of all the stupid things to do.

Papá insisted she come along, that a wedding celebration would get her away from the musty books and rotting manuscripts she loves so much, give her a chance to see more of the kingdom. "She is your heir, after all," he said. "Until you produce one of your own. She could use the experience of a diplomatic journey."

But Elisa has shown as much interest in ruling as the team

of horses pulling her carriage, and Papá is at a loss about what to do with her. No matter that she is God's chosen, the first in a hundred years to bear his sacred stone. God nested it in her belly, like a berry shoved into a soft muffin, as a sign that she will one day perform an act of heroic service.

It's laughable. And a little bit sad. People like the ones we've seen on this journey, who have been harried by poor harvests and enemy skirmishes, could use a hero. The servants mutter that maybe God picked the wrong sister.

These thoughts swim in my head as our procession continues, eating away at my heart and mind like deadly poison. I must get them under control. This state visit is the important thing, and I have to be at my best.

I search my entourage for Lord Zito, the man who taught me much of what I know about the conde and this region, for he has not returned to my side after leaving it to aid my sister. His horse is easily recognizable by the spear jutting from a guidon cup attached to his saddle, and I spy it off to the side in a plowed field. I watch, puzzled, as Zito dismounts and crouches in a furrow. He grabs a handful of soft dirt, crumbles it between his fingers, sniffs it, *tastes* it.

"Stop," I tell my driver. The command echoes up and down the line. The stamp of boots ceases, and the wheels of the carriage creak to stillness.

"Lord Zito," I call out. "Does mountain dirt taste better than dirt in the capital?"

But Zito does not smile. "What do you see here, Your Highness? Look around you."

His voice is high-pitched and girlish. During the last war with Invierne, he was barely more than a boy when his service brought him an injury that left him a eunuch. But it also brought him the king's favor, which resulted in his appointment as my steward. I haven't had a nurse since Elisa was born. Papá knew by the time I could walk that I would be like a son to him, and only a personal steward would do.

I look around, trying to see what Zito sees. Though he is prone to these impromptu teaching moments, he has never been so graceless as to instruct me within hearing of my entire entourage. Whatever he has noticed must be very important indeed.

The fields are plowed but barren, with only a few sickly sprouts poking from the soil. The pastures are still brown from winter. On the terraced slopes that rise beyond, orchards that should be covered in blossoms show only stunted blooms. The trees covering the hills are a web of bony branches, yet to bud.

"Spring is a tardy guest to its mountain home," I say.

"Spring does not arrive *this* late," he says, and his words would not alarm me were it not for the deadly seriousness in his voice.

"A drought?" I say.

He straightens and brushes the dirt from his hands, then holds his palms out so I can see the muddy streaks. It is far from drought-dusty.

"The last time I saw fields like this, it was damage of my own doing," he says. "I salted a village the Inviernos settled on our side of the mountains. But there is no taste of salt here."

"So what is causing it?"

He shrugs, but I know it is not the casual gesture it appears. "We should discuss it later," he says. Privately, he means.

My gaze sweeps the mountainsides again, and now the rocky outcrops and dense stands of naked trees seem ominous.

Zito remounts and gestures the column forward, commanding them toward Khelia Castle with all haste. I sit back on the bench, lost in thought. No wonder the people seem so desperate and distrustful. How long have their fields been bare? Perhaps they've been feeling the sting of the king's neglect even more than I realized. And maybe open carriages, which provide access even to small children, were a bad idea after all.

2

WE have only a single league left to travel, but it takes hours over these poor roads. I'm so eager to reach Khelia and ask the conde about the blight on his land that I would abandon the carriages and supply wagons to ride ahead if I could. Alas, my sister fears horses and would rather cut off an arm than ride any distance.

We have not gone far when a great crack sounds. I twist in my seat and watch horrified as Elisa's carriage tips dangerously and one of its wheels tumbles down the mountainside. Guards grab the carriage and strain to keep it from toppling after. A trunk slips its ties and slides off the luggage shelf to bounce down the rocky slope, spilling garments as it goes. I breathe relief when Elisa and Ximena scramble out of the carriage to safety.

The guards work quickly to divest the carriage of its remaining cargo and divvy it up among the packhorses. Still, it's too long before we're ready to proceed, and I want to scream with frustration over the delay.

I scoot over on my bench to make room, and Elisa and Ximena climb into my own carriage, which Zito surrounds with a thicket of guards. Most are devout followers of the path of God, and I saw how quick they were to defend her from a potential mob, how quick to grab her carriage and get her to safety. If danger comes to us both, I wonder, would they be more ready to protect their chosen one than their crown princess?

Elisa settles across from me and leans back against the thin cushions. Strands of hair have escaped her braid; they curl around her face, which is damp from sweat. Her plump cheeks are blotched red as apples. Ximena tirelessly fans Elisa with a browned palm leaf. After a while, the dry rustling is like an itch on my brain. I despair of ever being free of the sound.

"Will we be there soon, do you think?" Elisa says wearily.

"I asked Papá to loan us his *winged* carriage, but it was at the coach wright's for repairs," I answer.

"There's no need to be mean," Elisa says. "I'm not complaining." She closes her eyes, turning her sweating face to take the best advantage of Ximena's fanning. "This blight on the countryside worries me," she adds. "If we get there early enough, I can spend some time praying for the conde and his bride before we are whisked away for formal appearances. I've tried to in the carriage, but it's just too hot. My Godstone . . ." She opens her eyes and regards me steadily. "You know how it warms when I pray."

She seems to have an endless supply of subtle and creative

ways to remind me that even though I will be queen someday, *she* is God's chosen one. The words are out of my mouth before I can stop them: "Oh, I know better than to expect you to *do* anything once we arrive. Just hurry off to pray or rest. Let me handle the business of representing Papá."

Elisa flinches. Nurse Ximena gives me a sharp look.

I turn my head, guilt pricking my chest. Fury is like a monster inside me, the one thing in my life I've been unable to master. I send up a quick prayer of apology. *I know you don't listen to me the way you listen to my sister. But I'm sorry just the same.* And then, because I am me and not my sister, I add: *Of course if you would help me see the strength in her, or nudge her to be a little more useful, then I wouldn't have to be sorry.*

Very likely this is why my prayers are seldom answered.

When the castle finally comes into view—much later in the day than I had hoped—I stare in astonishment. Lord Zito's descriptions have not prepared me for the sight.

Khelia rises on a huge spur of granite that overlooks the confluence of two rivers: the Hinder, which pours from the jungle-choked mountains to the south, and the Crowborn, a rocky spine twisting down from the Sierra Sangre that flows wet only three seasons out of the year. The castle walls come together in a point—like the prow of a ship cresting the green waves of the jungle canopy. Three towers rise up in a line behind it, like the ship's mast stumps.

Elisa is as wide-eyed as I am. "According to legend," she says, "Khelia was built thousands of years ago by a rich admiral around the wreck of his warship when a great sea dried up."

That's my sister. Fond of useless knowledge. "Just stories," I reply. "Repeated by simple people to explain the castle's unique profile."

"Perhaps. But the foundations *are* ancient, much older than the walls. Some say the Inviernos built it. Even the name of the castle is thought to come from an Invierno word."

I shrug. "The importance of Khelia is that it watches over a crossroads. To the east lies Invierne—"

"And to the south," Elisa interrupts, "in the jungle of the Hinders, the Perditos crouch like vultures, ready to strip anyone or anything to the bone. The walls of Khelia, and the soldiers stationed here, guard Orovalle from these threats. I am not *stupid*, Alodia."

Whisk, whisk, whisk. Ximena waves the fan, giving no indication that she witnesses yet another argument. She has become adept over the years at turning a deaf ear to them.

As the carriage winds up the long road to the peak, the castle wall looms over us, seemingly impregnable. It is lucky this castle stands guard on Orovalle's behalf. I intend to make sure it continues to do so.

Papá, you have been foolish to neglect Paxón for so long.

Trumpets rend the sky with the first measures of the "Entrada Triunfal." The carriage passes through a massive wooden gate into a tiled courtyard surrounded by high adobe walls. I brace myself for the inevitable thunder of cheering that always greets me on state visits.

But there is only silence.

The citizens of the castle fill the wide courtyard in neat

little groups arranged by status and rank. Directly across from us, the conde and his bride-to-be stand with their stewards, servants, and extended families. Behind them are rows of craftsmen, draftsmen, farmers, and children—their faces scrubbed, wearing their finest clothes.

None of them seem happy to see us.

To our right stand two dozen knights wearing Paxón's crest—a golden ship on an emerald green background. A hundred liveried soldiers stand behind them. To our left are a dozen armed guards wearing polished armor more in the style of Joya d'Arena, our neighbor beyond the Hinders. The small group of soldiers backing them is made up of battle-scarred veterans.

We are supposedly among allies. But I can't help thinking that both the crown princess and the bearer of the Godstone are flanked and outnumbered.

"Elisa," I say quietly, keeping my expression neutral. "I know you don't feel well. You and Ximena should go to the chapel and pray. I'll make excuses for you." *Pray that I have misread this situation.*

"Don't be afraid, dear sister," Elisa says, and for a moment I imagine that she knows exactly what I am thinking. But no, she remains as blind to subtle—and not so subtle—social cues as ever. "I won't embarrass you. Let's go meet them."

She hops down from the carriage and walks straight into the lion's mouth.

3

THE moment my feet touch ground, everyone in the courtyard kneels. Zito holds out his arm to escort me, and together we move toward the conde in what I hope is a stately and dignified manner. With his other hand, Zito uses his spear like a cane, and the *tap-tap* echoes throughout the courtyard.

When we reach the conde and his lady, Zito waves back the herald and announces us himself. "Her Royal Highness Juana-Alodia de Riqueza, Crown Princess of Orovalle and the Jewel of the Golden Valley. Her Royal Highness Lucero-Elisa de Riqueza."

I offer my ring, and the conde kisses it, showing neither eagerness nor reluctance. "Rise," I say. The conde stands, and everyone with him.

I try to ignore the sounds of armor shifting, the quiet rattle of swords.

"Your Highness," Zito says. "I present Conde Paxón, Castellan of Khelia, Guardian of Crowborn Crossing, and a First Knight of the Crown."

The conde is a man of middle age, with pain lines on his face that belie his trim, active-looking figure. A brace imprisons his right leg, the one mauled by a boar. Even so, he noticeably leans to his left, keeping his full weight off it.

"Welcome, Your Highness," Paxon says. "We are honored that you have come all this way to share in our celebration."

"The honor is ours," I reply. He smiles in response, but never have I seen a man who seemed less likely to celebrate. The lady beside him keeps her eyes lowered, but her face is red and blotched. From crying? "And this is?"

"This is Lady Calla de Isodel," he says. He indicates the older couple standing behind her and adds, "And these are her parents, Lord Jorán and Lady Aña de Isodel."

Even at a distance, Lord Jorán's oiled beard reeks of myrrh; he must be very wealthy indeed. His wife is expertly coifed and lightly rouged, though she lowers her eyes and slumps her shoulders, impressively achieving a meek mildness that blurs her beauty.

"I was intrigued by the name Isodel when I saw it on the invitation," I say. It's not a place I'd heard of before, which was odd, as I've memorized my kingdom's geography down to every last hillock. Before setting off on our journey, I found it necessary to look up references to Isodel in the monastery archive. I'm curious how the people will represent themselves to the crown. "Do tell me about it," I say.

My question is directed at the young bride, for I wish to take her measure. But her father steps in front of her and says, "Your Highness, you have not heard of it because Isodel is like a flipped coin, falling sometimes on one side and sometimes on the other, according to chance—"

"Lady Calla?" I interrupt, and I'm not sure which irritates me more: his assumption that I would travel here in ignorance, or his refusal to let his daughter speak.

Lady Calla glances at her father, shamefaced, then back to me. It's the first clear look I have of her face. She is lovely enough to make other young women insane with envy, but unlike that of her cowed mother, hers is not a sheltered beauty. Her face is tan from the sun, and laugh lines spread from the corners of her eyes, though no trace of a smile touches her features now.

"Isodel is a small holding in the Hinders," she says at last. "Near the merchant road, surrounded by terraced orchards and herds of sheep. As my father said, sometimes it falls on one side of the border, sometimes on the other. Joya d'Arena currently claims our land, but King Alejandro has not sent his tax collectors our way in many years. That would not be so bad, but he has not sent his soldiers either, and Perditos threaten our trade." She glances at her betrothed, and Conde Paxón gives her an encouraging nod. "Without a good marriage, it will not matter who claims Isodel—there will be nothing left."

I'm delighted at her forthrightness and her concise appraisal. But her father glowers, and her mother coughs discreetly into her hand. I'm about to break the awkward silence with an inane observation about the weather when a door slams. An unkempt girl of about ten, sun darkened and wind burned, dashes across the courtyard toward us.

"Tía Calla, Tía Calla!" she cries. A young nursemaid pursues her, but when she sees me, she falls to her knees, muttering apologies.

Not so the girl, who runs to Calla's side. Her knees are badly scuffed. Nettles cling to her hair and hems, and her slippers are caked with dried mud.

"Lupita!" Lady Calla says with a pointed look. "This is the royal princess Alodia. You must curtsy to her and say 'Your Highness' and wait until she bids you rise."

I expect an ill-behaved protest, but the untidy girl shows extraordinary grace, curtsying swiftly and perfectly. "Your Highness," she intones with grave seriousness, though mischief dances in her eyes.

"Rise, Lupita."

She jumps up as swiftly as she knelt, and looks back and forth between Calla and Elisa. "Is she the one? Are you the one? Are you the bearer of the Godstone? Can I see it?"

There are a few nervous titterings, but Elisa addresses the child calmly. "A lady never shows such things in public."

Lupita nods. "But have you come to save us?"

Elisa's face freezes, and I squirm with embarrassment for her. The thought of my sister saving anyone is absurd, a fact of which she is too well aware.

I'm dying to ask what they need saving from, but Lord Zito steps forward and says, "Conde, the sun is setting. Perhaps it would be best to continue this conversation inside."

4

ZITO, Elisa, Ximena, and I follow the conde and his mayordomo to the audience hall, which is dimly lit by grimy clerestory windows. The dry air smells faintly of incense. Dusty tables are scattered haphazardly throughout, covered with cold candles in various states of melt. It feels like a place that suffers human company rarely—a good place for secrets, perhaps.

Zito leans over and whispers, "You shamed Lady Calla's father."

"He shamed himself," I whisper back. "But I don't care about him. Unless *he* is the reason everyone seems so anxious? Or is it the blight on the land that has the castle on edge?"

"Maybe His Grace will tell us."

"His Grace will tell you what?" We turn at the sound of the conde's voice. He has edged closer to us, using his cane for support.

Zito says, "I observed that your father-in-law seems tense and unhappy, and Her Highness asked me why this might be."

"It's a complicated situation," Paxón says.

The mayordomo leads us all to a mahogany table with matching chairs that creak their age as we sit.

Paxón asks the mayordomo to fetch refreshments. He stretches out his bad leg, then takes a deep breath and says, "This wedding was intended as a bold stroke, princess, a way of strengthening my countship's border. With the Perditos to the south and the Inviernos to the east both growing audacious, I hoped to acquire a strong ally in the Hinders. I had also hoped . . ." His face turns sheepish. "That such a bold move would gain the attention and interest of your father. I want him to understand that we continue to take our duty of guarding Orovalle's border quite seriously."

A surge of triumph fills me, but I tamp it down. Such a gesture will require something in return from the crown, something to assure Paxón that he remains a valued vassal. One thing is certain: I *will* see this wedding done. It fits so neatly into my plans to shore up the region in preparation for my own reign.

The conde has fallen silent and thoughtful. "But?" I prompt.

"But . . . ever since Lady Calla and her family have arrived here, so that we might get to know one another before we wed, we have been cursed. We have lost God's favor."

I try not to gape at him. "Strong words. The *Scriptura Sancta* says, 'It is not for man to know the intent of God.'" I glance over at Elisa to see if she notices my thinly veiled message, but if she does, she hides it well.

"And yet the signs are there," the conde says. "We've plowed our fields and planted our seeds, but nothing sprouts. The trees refuse to blossom."

Elisa leans forward. "Many things affect the arrival of God's bounty," she says. "Rain, cold, and so on."

Paxón shakes his head. "We have been touched by neither late frost nor early drought. Indeed, the weather this year has been just short of perfect. But nothing grows. Almost everything that sustains this castle comes from within a league of its walls, but everything within a league is dead, save for the wild, uncultivated jungle that abuts our southern wall."

"It does seem unnatural," I concede.

Paxón winces at the word, but he does not deny it. "Lord Jorán has expressed doubts about going through with the wedding. He fears God's wrath. Thus far Isodel remains untouched, but if it is some kind of blight, it is bound to spread. Besides that, all these extra guests have depleted our stores, which we expected to replenish with early crops. Fights have broken out between Lord Jorán's soldiers and my own. And then . . ." He pauses, runs a hand through his hair.

I exchange a worried look with Zito. "And then?" I say.

"There is Espiritu," he says.

"Espiritu?" Elisa asks. "What is that?"

"He appeared about a month ago," Paxón says. "They call him Espiritu for the way he slips into sheep pens and chicken coops and melts away with his prey. He makes no sound, leaves no mark save for an occasional drop of blood or a scattering of feathers. But they hear him in the night, screaming at the moon in rage and heartbreak. Our soldiers have searched the hills for him, but they find only empty cottages, marked with signs of blood and violence."

"A jaguar, maybe?" Elisa says. "Man-eaters are rare, but not unknown. There was a pair that worked together, terrorizing the northern holdings for several years before they were hunted down and killed."

"How do *you* know about the shadow cats, Your Highness?" says Paxón, and I don't appreciate the mockery in his tone. "Have you hunted them yourself?"

"I . . . I've read about them. I read a lot."

"Then let me tell you some things that you will not find in books. Our seamstress was working just the other night, sewing a flounce onto Lady Calla's wedding *terno* by candlelight. Espiritu screamed, sending shivers through her heart. When she awoke in the morning, she discovered the flounce's seam had gone crooked, the stitches slipped, as if even the *terno* could not bear Espiritu's jagged grief."

"Well, perhaps she should not sew by candlelight," Elisa says. But my skin prickles.

Paxón continues, undeterred. "And two nights ago, when the ostler was oiling the tack for my mount, the one I'll ride in the wedding procession, the great cat screamed again and panicked the horses. It took half the night to soothe them. In the morning, the ostler discovered that rats had fouled the last of the oats and the barrel of apples had gone to rot."

"How can the cry of a great cat do that?" Elisa says. "It

is more likely caused by the same thing that poisoned your fields."

I wince. Elisa possesses all the subtlety of a cudgel. "My dear sister," I say. "Let us respect their wisdom in these matters. Perhaps Espiritu *is* the instrument of God's judgment."

Ximena lays a hand on Elisa's arm, but my sister ignores her. "But what is being done here that God would wish to cast judgment on?" she says.

"The wedding, maybe?" says the conde. "Though why—"

The door cracks open, and Lady Calla and Lupita enter, followed by the little girl's nurse, who is anxiously wringing her hands.

"Please join us, Lady Calla," I say, indicating an empty chair.

Calla pushes the little girl ahead of her. She has donned a clean dress, and most of the wildness has been brushed from her hair, though she still wears the mud-covered slippers. I smile to think of the many times Zito or my attendants tried to clean me up in a hurry, only to discover later that they had missed a bit of bramble or a pair of slippers.

"We are sorry for interrupting you," Calla says. "Guadalupe-Esteva, go on now. Apologize to the princess."

I fold my hands in front of me, bemused. Maybe I will ask her to serve as my personal page while I am here.

She walks over to Elisa and drops into a curtsy.

"I'm very sorry that I asked you personal questions, Your Highness," Lupita says. "It was . . ." She looks up at Lady

Calla and gets a nod of encouragement. "It was *disrespectful* and *inappropriate*," she finishes.

"You are forgiven," Elisa tells her graciously, with no reprimand and no instruction.

Just like that. My jaw clenches. It is well and good to be so indulgent, to never demand recriminations or consequences, when one does not have to consider the responsibilities of ruling.

"Are you excited about the wedding?" Elisa asks the little girl.

"I was supposed to be a flower girl, but there are no flowers."

"We'll find some dried flowers for you to carry," Calla says, resting her hand on the girl's head.

"They aren't the same," Lupita says.

"No, they aren't," Elisa says, pulling something from the little girl's hair. "Where did this nettle come from?"

"By the creek," Lupita says.

"And I bet there were red flowers on those stems," Elisa says. "Scarlet hedge nettle is so tough that nothing can stop it from blooming. I saw huge clumps of it on our way here."

"It's just a weed," Lupita says.

"It's a *beautiful* weed," Elisa answers. "And the perfect flower for you to carry, for it is like the people of Khelia, strong and unstoppable, capable of blooming and thriving where nothing else can grow."

I study my sister thoughtfully. I didn't even notice the flowers she speaks of.

"You may gather some tomorrow," Calla says. "Now it is time for bed."

She gestures for the nurse to lead Lupita away. The girl practically bounces out the door, listing all the places she has seen scarlet hedge nettle.

"Thank you for your kindness to my niece," Calla says, addressing both of us. "Her mother, my sister, died several years ago. Lupita has become very special to me."

"To both of us," Paxón says softly. The look they exchange is one of understanding and affection. Rulers rarely get to marry those they care for. There is certainly no love match in *my* future, and I am a bit envious of them. It leaves me feeling even more determined to see this wedding through.

The mayordomo returns with a tray of savory pastries: small puffs filled with diced mushrooms, cheese and chive scones, and tiny quiches with red pepper. Elisa downs a handful of the mushroom puffs before I've made my first selection, and I glance around, a bit embarrassed, but no one else seemed to notice.

We speak of small, safe topics for a while, such as last winter's unusually low snowline, the growing price of lumber, and whether or not Ventierra wine is the finest in the world. I'm glad for the opportunity to ignore the tension around us and be merely pleasant together. As a child, I found such exchanges tedious and awful, but lately I've come to appreciate the power of a seemingly senseless conversation to establish trust and heal relationships. I'm about to ask how Paxón and Calla first met when Elisa rises from her chair.

"I'd like to spend some time praying tonight," she says. "If you'll all excuse me . . ." Everyone stands when she does, and I'm torn between frustration at her gracelessness and relief that she will soon be gone, leaving me to finesse everything without her interference.

I'm leaning forward to give her a formal kiss on the cheek when the cat screams.

It's high-pitched and wild, like breaking glass and deepest anguish. My whole body turns to gooseflesh, and my heart kicks at my ribs like a panicked horse trying to break from its stall. I'm not the only one so affected. We all stand frozen for the span of several heartbeats.

Paxón is the first to collect himself, and his face is pale as a ghost's as he says, "It came from the eastern garden. Inside the—"

A woman screams.

5

THE conde rushes us through the halls. We are joined in our dash by household staff and watch soldiers. Paxón shouts at everyone to move aside and let us pass.

The walled garden is perfectly square and small, not much larger than my private suite at home. In the center looms an enormous tree whose canopy shades the entire garden. It's the kind of place where I would have played as a little girl, especially during the hottest days of summer, when Zito forbade me to absorb too much sunshine lest it darken my skin.

Tucked against the wall is a stone sculpture of a crouching jaguar. The flickering torchlight casts random shadows, making it seem as if the tail moves, as if the cat is ready to pounce. The sight sends another chill up my spine, even before I realize that the wet blotches on the head and paws are blood.

Lupita's nurse is on her knees bawling, begging someone, anyone to help. She grasps a tiny muddy slipper in her left hand.

Calla looses a sob, and Paxón wraps her in his arms. A servant gestures wildly, explaining that he saw the shadow cat escaping as he rushed into the courtyard. A black-pelted demon, he says, that skimmed the wall with ghostly grace. Whispers of "Espiritu!" swirl around us.

"This makes no sense," Elisa mutters. She stares at the blood, eyes glazed. "This is not how jaguars act." My sister has never seen so much blood, so much violence. It must be even more of a shock to her than the rest of us. Before I realize what I'm doing, I lift an arm to drape around her shoulders. But she stiffens, and I let the arm drop.

The men are organized by their captains and prepare to search in the dark. Several of our own guards look to Zito, asking permission to join up, and he grants it. Paxón shouts that there will be a reward for anyone who returns Lupita to her aunt.

Lord Zito grasps my shoulder. "Are you all right, Highnesses?" he asks, looking into each of our faces.

"Nothing here is right," I say, shaking my head. The pool of blood at the foot of the sculpture is smeared by footprints, the wall above it streaked with crimson. "So much blood," I murmur.

"Too much," he says. "I doubt the girl lives."

My heart squeezes, and I realize that I had warmed to the girl—her brightness and energy—and hardly knew it. "The men must search for her anyway," I say. "They need a purpose, something to do so they don't fight with one another."

"And there's a chance, isn't there, Zito?" Elisa asks in a

small voice. "A slight chance that she still lives?"

He nods. "But we also need to think ahead," he says gently. "It would be indelicate to bring it up now with the conde, but we must consider that Lady Calla's father is unlikely to allow the wedding to proceed if the girl is not found."

Zito and I exchange a grim look. As war with Invierne looms, Papá and I must do all we can to strengthen this, our weakest border. The wedding must go on. But I have no idea how.

6

I cannot sleep, not while the soldiers are out searching. I stand on the wall and watch their torches wink and flash as they wind through the hills. And I'm still awake long after midnight, when the last of the men returns empty-handed. The wedding is scheduled to take place the sunrise after this one, but based on the crying and arguing that rings through the castle late into the night, I am certain it will be canceled.

A sense of failure weighs on me. I need to *do* something.

While my servants sleep, I dress quietly in riding breeches and a stiff leather vest that is fitted to my body like a second skin. My calfskin boots won't protect my feet as well as my riding boots, but they make it easier to step soundlessly. I don't know yet exactly where I'm going or what I'm doing, but Lord Zito has trained me to be prepared.

My feet carry me to the place where Lupita disappeared. Someone is already in the garden when I arrive, someone whose profile I recognize even in the dark, long before I see the spear he leans upon.

"Lord Zito."

He jumps as if I've startled him from deep thought. Bowing his head, he says, "Your Highness."

"What brings you here?"

"I couldn't sleep for thinking of the girl. Everyone is too shocked, too grieved. I'm trying to see this place with clearer eyes."

"Explain."

He gestures toward the sculpture. "For one thing, there's too much blood. Jaguars kill by piercing the skulls of their prey, not by draining them of blood. And look here. See this second scrape of blood on the wall? Too far away from the first. Were there two cats? He couldn't have carried the girl over the wall twice."

That's what Elisa was saying. She wasn't shocked; she was thinking. "So you agree with my sister?"

"I do. And you would do well to heed her. She reads widely and wisely, and knows an uncanny amount about those things with which she has little personal experience."

It is more praise for my sister than I am accustomed to hearing. "Reading can only take you so far, up to the moment where you must take action with your own hands."

He nods, which makes me feel relieved, though I'm not sure why.

"Let's do it, then," I say. "You and I. Let's take action."

"We will. The cooks are already up preparing breakfast, and our guard will be ready to resume the search as soon as the sun is above the horizon."

"And their noise will drive off the jaguar or send it into hiding so that we have no chance of finding it. We must look now, while the countryside is undisturbed."

"*Princesita*," he says. It's a diminutive he uses only when pleading with me, as he did when my heart was broken the first—and last—time, and I climbed out a window to the edge of the roof to mourn in private. He thought I was going to jump.

"The jaguar will be drowsy," I say. *Because it has eaten its fill.* Zito winces. "If we bring the cat back, destroy this thing that has everyone so terrified, they'll see us as heroes. Saviors. We might even save this wedding. At the very least, we'll demonstrate that the crown still cares about Paxón's people."

"Alodia, please," he says.

"Are you coming with me?" I say. I climb onto the back of the stone jaguar, careful to avoid the drying blood, and it's only a short reach to pull myself atop the wall. But the garden is built into a slope, and the drop on the other side is longer than I anticipated. I hesitate.

"Here," he says, a bit angrily. "If you're going out there by yourself, you'll need a weapon." He pulls a knife from his belt and tosses it up to me. I snatch it from the air.

He means to discourage me, but he has failed. I slip the blade into my own belt. "Thank you. I'll see you when I return, then."

I swing my legs over the wall, then my body, and hang by my fingertips. The drop between my boots and the ground is little more than the height of a man, but in the dark, it feels like a chasm.

"Alodia!" The whispered exclamation is accompanied by

the soft thud of his staff and the sound of his boots on the sculpture.

It is all I need to hear. I let go.

My legs are too stiff when I hit the ground. The impact shivers up to my knees, which respond by buckling, and I plop gracelessly onto my rear.

"Are you all right, Highness?"

"Come find me if I'm not back by the noon meal."

He mutters something under his breath that I'm fairly certain is a string of swear words in several languages, and then says, "Move away from the wall. I'm coming down."

I'm glad the dark hides my smile as I scramble out of his way. His spear drops first, clacking against the wall before it hits the ground. He follows a moment later, rolling upon impact, and comes up standing. I am impressed.

He brushes off his pants. "Your Highness, this is foolish beyond measure, even for you."

I hand him his spear. My left ankle hurts a little when I shift my weight onto it, but I'll never tell. "You said something does not add up, and I agree. Let's trace the creature's path, and see if we can find what has eluded us."

One thing I have learned from many years of watching my father is that some people, the best ones, are motivated more by the chance to prove themselves than by a command to serve. It is the work itself that calls them onward, especially if they believe they are the only ones who can do it.

"Zito, you're the smartest man I know. I *need* your help with this."

His eyes narrow with suspicion, but even he is not immune to such persuasion. "Just a quick look," he says.

I have won. Grinning, I turn and hike into the jungle, following the faint deer trail an animal might take if it landed on the ground at this spot.

"Let's go this way," he says as he catches up with me, but I see the direction he is pointing and will have none of it.

"That would take us down toward the river and the village. Jaguars are creatures that retreat upward, into the mountains, into the trees."

His answering sigh makes me laugh. "It was worth a try."

Hours later, I'm beginning to recognize this trek as foolhardiness. I hate giving up on anything, but we've seen no sign of the cat, and my ankle is swelling. I'm about to suggest we turn back when we come face-to-face with a steep slope of loose rock, marked by dark spots that might be caves or shadows or pockets of vegetation. The air is still—too still. No birds sing, even though the sun now edges the eastern horizon.

"A good hiding place for a shadow cat, wouldn't you say?" I whisper.

"Maybe," he answers, his voice wary.

"We should look for scat or prints, then report back to—"

The jaguar's cry, right on top of us, freezes me to the bone. A black shadow separates from an overhead branch and leaps. Zito crashes to the ground.

7

ZITO rolls with the jaguar, striking it with his spear. "Run, Alodia!"

I spin. My ankle catches in a root, and I hear a great crack like splintering wood. I scream, falling to my knees. Through a haze of tears and a red curtain of pain, I see death leaping toward me. The jaguar has abandoned Zito to attack me.

I fumble for the knife. I pull it from my belt and yank off the sheath, which I fling at the jaguar with a cry of fury. It bats aside the piece of leather with a giant paw the way a man swats a harmless mosquito. It leaps, but I roll, and the snapping jaws barely miss my neck; the raking claws slide off my leather vest.

The cat lands behind me, and I barely have time to twist on the ground to face it before it is on me again, forcing the air from my lungs with the weight of its body.

I grab a fistful of fur and flesh at its throat and, with strength born of desperation, hold the jaws at bay just enough to avoid having my skull crushed. Its warm breath reeks of sour meat, and one fang is dark with rot. The cat snarls as it rolls its head, trying to pull loose from my grasp. Claws rake my shoulder, trailing white-hot pain.

But I do not let go, and I stab wildly at its face, over and over, until the knife slides into a yellow eye. The jaguar roars, wrenching its head, yanking the knife away. I grab for the hilt, trying to reclaim it, but the massive cat collapses on top of me.

I pound at the animal with my fists. Seconds or minutes pass until I realize the creature is limp and dead. I manage to shift a little, just enough to fill my chest with air. A sob of joy at deliverance wracks my body.

After collecting my breath, I try to shove the cat aside, but I can't. I start to leverage my way out, but I scream the moment my ankle pushes against the ground.

My tears dissolve into laughter. I have killed the jaguar, but it may yet kill me.

A shadow passes over me. Then, a grunt. The cat is flung aside.

"Zito!"

"Alodia! Are you—?"

He crouches beside me and peers toward my wounded shoulder. It's probably bleeding badly. I hardly care. "Zito, I thought you were . . ." I can't even say it.

"*You* were its target," he says. "It saw you limping and pegged you as easy prey." I wince as he pushes back my sleeve to get a better look. "Poor creature—it had no idea who it was tangling with."

"We have to cut open the cat's stomach," I say. "We have to find out if it . . ."

He nods, wrenches his knife from the cat's head, and expertly slits open its belly. Organs spill out, steaming and stinking. He grabs the white-pink stomach and slices it open. The contents ooze out, like stew from a cracked bowl. I don't know what I expect to see—the girl's body, her face, her other muddied shoe—but none of it is there.

Zito pokes through the mess with the knife. "This hunter has not been eating well. I see a feather. Small rodent bones."

"Then whose blood was in the garden?"

He shrugs for an answer, shifts to the other side of the creature, and stares at its hindquarters. A faint rosette pattern is barely visible in its matted black fur. "There's an arrow deep in its haunch," Zito says. "It was the hunted, not the hunter. Maybe it leaped into the garden to escape. The blood smears were the jaguar's, not the girl's." After a pause, he adds, "You were lucky, Alodia. If the cat had not been injured and starving, you may not have been able to handle it."

It's getting harder to think as the fear and fury of battle dissipate, leaving only agonizing pain in their place. "That doesn't make sense," I manage. "If anyone in the village shot it, they would have raised the alarm."

I don't like the look that passes across Zito's face.

He thrusts the knife into the cat's flank, digging and prying. Blood oozes slowly now that the cat is dead, disappearing into the thick black fur and leaving a sticky sheen. A moment later, Zito pulls out an arrowhead. A string of muscle sways from the serrated edge. The shaft has been chewed off.

"Zito?"

"This is an Invierno arrowhead," he whispers, and his eyes lift and scan the surrounding area. "That would explain what drove the jaguar out of the mountains. And perhaps more than that. We need to get back to Khelia Castle immediately."

But it's too late. Speak of evil, and you summon it. Voices filter through the jungle.

"It came from over there," comes a clipped voice.

"The cat is long gone by now," says another.

"The whole castle was out looking for it last night. They'll come again. We need to find that arrow before they do."

Zito and I must escape. But I'm in no condition to go anywhere.

8

ZITO slips his arm under mine and pulls me up. "Pray there is a cave or shelter among those rocks," he whispers. He places the hilt of the knife in my mouth. "Bite down. Do not cry out."

The taste of jaguar blood makes me choke, but I swallow the bile as it rises. Zito leans on his spear, dragging me along as fast as he can manage.

The trees conceal us, but my foot dangles uselessly. It snags on a root, sending us both sprawling. The knife cuts my cheek as I slam the hard earth, but I do not cry out. I will not cry out.

A startled exclamation filters through the trees as the bandits find the dead jaguar.

Zito lifts me again, sees the blood on my face, and slides the knife into his belt. We limp onward, with barely two good legs between us. My head throbs. I hear him talking to me, as if from far away.

"This is well concealed," he says. "Hard to reach, hard to find."

He drags me forward, and the world goes black. My next sense is that we are halfway up a sloping wall of rock and scrub. Zito no longer carries his spear. One arm is wrapped around me; the other pulls both of us upward.

I hate this. I hate the fear. I hate that I must be helped.

Darkness looms. At first I take it for a shadow, but my hazing vision clears to reveal a small cave, just large enough for me to crawl inside.

"You go first," I say. "Pull me in."

"Shhh," he whispers, gently easing me sideways into the narrow opening. "Hide here. I'll run back to the castle and bring help."

I grab his arm. "I'll go with you."

"No." He hands me the knife, hilt first.

"You'll need it if they catch up to you!"

We hear voices in the distance.

"I must run," he says, pulling the knife back with reluctance. "Stay quiet. Stay *alive*. I'll be back."

And just like that, he slips away. Tears well up in my eyes. I tell myself it's from the pain. That's the first thing I must do, then. Bind my ankle. Immobilize it and stop the swelling.

I scoot farther back into the cave, where the higher ceiling allows me to sit upright. The sun is above the horizon now. Enough light filters in that I can see my ankle.

It would be better if I could not. It is purple and swollen, and my foot turns at an odd angle. It's not broken—it's dislocated.

I've dislocated fingers several times. There is nothing to

do but yank them back into place and bind them up until they heal. Surely the principle is the same with an ankle. The good news is that the pain will be much diminished once I accomplish it. It might even support my weight, should it come to that. I unlace my boots, then brace my foot against the wall. I lean over and press my fingertips into the swollen skin, looking for the right grip. Red spots dance in my vision.

I take three deep breaths and shove my ankle into place. Bone scrapes bone. The cave darkens.

When I come to, I am dizzy and my vision is blurry, so it is a full second before I realize the shadow leaning over me is a person. I prepare to strike, hard and fast, when a small hand covers my mouth.

A girl's hand. Lupita's hand.

"Your Highness," she whispers, her voice trembling.

"Lupita!" I grab her and hug her tight. "How did you—?"

"I'm sorry! I just wanted to find the scarlet hedge nettle. For the flowers—"

"I remember. You've been here all night?"

She buries her head in my chest. I stroke her hair.

"What happened, Lupita? Tell me. But do it quietly."

"Yes, Your Highness." She swallows hard. "I was going to look for flowers, climbing over the wall. And then . . . and then I heard . . ."

"Espiritu."

She nods.

"We have killed him, Lupita. He'll never hurt anyone again."

"He leaped onto the wall, and I was so scared. I jumped down and started to run. Then there were men in the woods. Perditos. I didn't know where I was going. I just ran and ran until I came here."

I marvel that this small child made the same drop that injured my ankle. "It's all right. Do you remember Lord Zito?"

"The man with the funny voice?"

"He's the one who brought me here. He is running back to the castle for help."

"I hope he is a very fast runner," she says. She gestures for me to come see, and I drag myself toward the opening.

The rising sun has revealed a small meadow between the cliffs and the jungle below. It holds a camp—the remains of a fire and some scattered supplies.

"They hid here last night, when the soldiers were searching. I wanted to sneak past them, but—"

"You were smart not to try. But no one is down there now."

She gasps and melts back into the shadow of the cave.

Men with faces painted black emerge from the trees. Bones from their anklets rattle as they walk. They wear clothes hacked from poorly tanned hides, and their hair hangs in clumps. Perditos.

But they are not alone.

A tall, thin man with long white hair and a supple cloak accompanies the bandits. The staff he carries bears a glowing jewel in an iron cage at its tip.

An Invierno. Not just an Invierno, but an animagus, one of their powerful sorcerers.

Behind him come two more Perditos, dragging someone else, and my heart is in my throat even before my mind makes sense of the scene.

They have captured my steward. He hangs limp between them, and blood drips from a gash on his forehead. *Oh, Zito.*

No rescue is forthcoming. It will be up to me to save us all.

9

"LUPITA, you must help me," I say. "I need you to bind up my ankle as tight as possible."

"How?" she whispers.

I start untying the stays on either side of my stiff leather vest. "With this. Here, help me get it off."

Her fingers are more nimble than mine, and her hands shake less. In a few moments, we have it off and the two pieces separated. The front piece is shaped oddly, the rawhide sculpted to my curves, but it has a little more flexibility than the back.

Outside, the Perditos argue loudly. I feel a desperate need to hurry, even if I don't know my next step.

"Now the sleeves of my shirt," I say. They are also held on with laces. I wince when Lupita's efforts scrape at my injured shoulder and breathe relief when she's done pulling the sleeves off my arms. I tie them together and wrap them crosswise around my ankle. I need three times their length, but it will have to do.

I grab the front half of my vest. "We need to roll this up. Leather armor is not very flexible, so you'll have to press hard." I show her what I mean and hand it to her. "We'll wrap it around my lower leg, as low as we can and as tight as we can, and then we'll tie it in place. Can you do that?"

"Yes—"

A scream of anguish echoes from below. Lupita's gaze darts outside; then she twitches toward the deeper part of the cave. She is confused, frightened, ready to go in every direction at once.

"Right here, stay with me, Lupita. I need you to be strong for me. Are you ready?"

Telling someone else to be strong is exactly what I need. When she nods, courage fills my own chest.

I unroll the vest just enough to slip it over my ankle, stifling a groan of pain. I take a deep breath. "Ready, Lupita? Make it as tight as you can. Don't be afraid to hurt me."

She presses down on the vest piece, rolling as she goes. "Harder," I tell her between gritted teeth. "Tighter."

When it's as tight as I can bear, I wrap the laces from my vest around it and knot them. I test the brace by pressing my foot against the cave wall. The pain is not nearly as bad as when the ankle was flopping uselessly.

The brace will do little to support it, but I hope it will shore up the exhausted muscles and tendons holding it in place. Maybe, just maybe, I'll be able to walk on it a little.

Lupita and I crawl back to the lip of the cave and peek outside, careful to keep our faces in the shadows. I wish we had not.

I cover the girl's mouth, but only to keep myself from screaming. Zito is on his knees, his arms bound behind him. One man holds him by the hair. Another places an arrow, its iron tip glowing red, against his blistering, blackening cheek. A bloody hole in his face marks the spot where Zito's right eye used to be.

The Perdito shifts the arrow tip to beneath his remaining eye.

"Who was with you, and where have they gone?" the Perdito says.

"It was the queen of Orovalle," Zito answers, laughing. "And she is a hawk, soaring above all of you."

The bandit presses the glowing arrowhead into Zito's cheek, and blood runs down his chin as he screams. Tears stream down my face.

"Look away, Lupita," I say. Her eyes are wide, and her shoulders shake. I turn her head against my chest and pull her close, then bury my face in her hair. "You should not see this."

"She is a horse no man can catch, galloping across the desert," Zito says. "She is—" He screams again.

"Pack everything up, we move out now," the Perdito says.

"Cut his throat," comes the animagus' slippery voice, and his preternatural calm is more chilling than all the rage in the world.

"Do it yourself, Chato," the Perdito leader answers. "Use him to work your blood magic. But *someone* was with him, so I suggest you make quick work of it before Paxón's men hunt us down."

I dare to peek from the cave's entrance. The Perdito gestures to the others to leave.

The animagus hisses, catlike, and the sound is so wild and inhuman that I shrink against the rock wall at my back. "The leash holding back the spring must be renewed daily," he says. "All our work is wasted if we leave now. The land will heal itself quickly."

"And all our work is wasted if we're dead," the Perdito says. Then he and his men melt into the jungle, opposite the direction of Khelia Castle.

The animagus glares after them a moment, then prods Zito with the end of his staff. My steward groans and twitches, and relief fills me.

I scramble backward, dragging Lupita with me. "Are you sneaky?" I whisper. "Are you fast?"

"Yes," she answers uncertainly.

"Espiritu is dead, and the bad men have gone away, all but that one. We cannot let him escape. I need you to run back to the castle and tell everyone."

She shakes her head. I understand her fear, but she must do this. I reach for her arm and give what I hope is a reassuring squeeze.

"You can sneak down on the shadowed side, hiding between the rocks. And then you must race back to the castle and tell your tía Calla everything."

"I'm scared."

"Of course you are. So am I. And Lady Calla is scared for you too. And your grandmother and grandfather. But

I cannot run back to the castle, not with my ankle. You're the only one who can do this. You must save your aunt by warning her about the Perditos."

I should hate myself for manipulating her this way, but I don't. I watch carefully as the fear on her face transmutes into something else. It's that same steely look Elisa gets when I'm about to scold her.

Not sullenness, I understand suddenly. Bravery.

Together we crawl to the lip of the cave. Zito sits in the center of the meadow, curled up on himself, panting. Around him, the animagus traces lines in the earth with the glowing end of his staff, a task that requires all his focus. I nod at Lupita and push her out of the cave. She freezes for just an instant, then turns and slips over the boulders as quietly as the moonrise.

I watch her go, ready to leap out after her if the animagus notices her, but she disappears into the jungle. I exhale relief, but it is short-lived. The animagus circles Zito as if in a trance, chanting as he drags his staff through the lines he drew, over and over again. They begin to glow with bluish light, and I feel sickness rise like a miasma from the earth. When it is done, I will have lost my chance to save my steward, however small it might be. My heart kicks in my chest.

I ease out from the cave and crouch among the boulders. My fingers close on a rock, the only weapon at hand. My ankle screams at me to stop, but I creep forward over the rocks as quickly and as quietly as I can. Gravel clatters down the slope. Surely he will hear. Surely he will look up.

I am not quick enough. The chant slows. The light in the animagus' staff blinks out. The glowing lines fade.

I've reached the meadow, but I'm too far away as he puts the knife to Zito's throat. I burst into a sprint, every stride an arrow of torment up my leg. But I will not falter. I will not fail.

The animagus whirls, eyes wide. He raises both staff and knife to defend himself.

I scream like the jaguar, raw and anguished, like a predator that will not be denied, and he freezes for the merest instance.

I leap and smash the rock across his head.

He falls, and I fall on top of him. I pound his head, feeling the bones crack underneath, until red and gray splash with each blow. I toss the bloody rock away, and grab the staff from his still-tight grip. I snap it across my knee, and throw the pieces into the underbrush.

Gasping, I hold my hands up to the light, shocked at the torrent of violence that flowed so easily from them. My knuckles bleed, and my right palm is scraped raw. I look down at the animagus' broken form, sickened at the mess I have made. And I watch, half in terror, half in relief, as his body shrivels before my eyes, like a piece of fruit left too long in the sun.

All the sickness and decay that flowed out of his ritual moments ago rushes back like a tide, flowing over and around me, until I am swimming in it. I fall to my hands and knees and vomit long past the time my stomach is empty.

The sickness fades, like mist dissipating in the warming

sun, leaving the scents of rich soil and moist bark and morning glory blooms. They are good scents. *Clean* scents.

"Zito," I say, crawling toward him because I cannot stand. "Zito."

"Alodia! What happened?" He turns his face to me, but the angle is not quite right, like he's looking at someone behind me.

I reach for his tied wrists. "Stop moving so I can untie you."

"Alodia," he whispers. "Just let me die."

"We're going back to the castle." His bonds are soaked in blood. My fingers fumble as I work the slimy knots.

"Without my eyes, what am I? Even less of a man than I was before."

I want to slap sense into him, but I am done hitting things today. Tears roll from my eyes. "Idiot. None of my guards are half the man you are. I can't make it without you."

"Alodia—"

"Shut up." My hands are shaking hard, but I finally untie the knots that bind his hands. "You're my best friend, Zito, and I need you."

"You don't need anyone," he says, rubbing his wrists.

"I need *you*," I repeat, wiping my nose on my bare arm. But such a declaration is too raw for me, no matter how true, so I add, "I can't walk on my own. I need you to lean on. Once we get back to the castle, you can crawl off and die." I find his spear on the ground and thrust it toward him. "So stop whining and get on your damn feet."

I can't tell if he's laughing or choking, and I don't care. He leverages himself up, then runs his hands along the length of his spear, as if getting to know it all over again.

He holds out his arm. "I can't see the way, Alodia," he says. "I suppose we need each other right now."

Half a dozen inappropriate replies jump to the tip of my tongue, but I keep my mouth firmly closed. We link arms and hobble back the way we came.

10

WE are nearly to the castle when something rustles through the underbrush ahead. I hear footsteps, and I'm about to yank Zito into a hollow of ferns when I also hear the creak of armor. The Perditos don't wear armor.

"Lupita?" I whisper.

Figures barrel down the deer path—four of my guards, Lupita, Nurse Ximena, and to my absolute shock, my little sister. Elisa's hair is full of dirt and leaves, her cheeks are flushed, and the hem of her gown is thick with mud, but she plows forward, her face set stubbornly. She holds a knife in her hand. A kitchen knife, I note with no small amount of amusement. What she thinks she'll do with it, I've no idea. When she sees me, her features melt into relief.

"What are you doing here?" I ask, and it comes out sharper than I intend.

It stops her cold. "I . . . well . . . I heard you leave last night. But then you didn't come back, and Zito was gone too. . . . And the cat screamed, so I fetched the guards, and then we found Lupita, and . . ." Something in my face makes her pause, and her own features harden in response. "I was worried for Zito. I know *you* can take care of yourself."

Lupita weaves through the guards toward me, then wraps my legs in a great hug, squeezing tight. I pat her head absently. "But why are *you* here? Why not send Khelia's guards?" How could she risk herself like this? She's the farthest thing from a warrior I've ever known. Of all the stupid . . . My anger dissolves. *No, my sister has never been stupid.*

"You left in secret," she whispers, fully cowed. "So, I knew you had a plan. You always have a plan. And I knew you would be so irritated with me if I spoiled it by telling everyone."

I stare at her, dismayed, because she is exactly right. "Elisa, I'm s—"

Zito places a silencing hand on my shoulder, probably thinking I'm about to scold her as usual. "Thank you for coming, Highness," he says. "And for bringing aid. It was quick thinking and brave."

Elisa gasps, as if seeing him for the first time. "Oh, my God," she says.

If she is just now noticing the blood dripping from his ruined eyes and the burn marks on his cheeks, then her only thought when undertaking this ridiculous rescue was for me. She truly thought she was rescuing *me.*

"We need to get Zito to the castle," I say, and my voice is gentler with her than it has been in a long time. "I'm worried about infection."

"Of course," she says. And my weak, lazy, selfish sister

clamps the silly kitchen knife between her teeth, hitches up her sleeves, and lodges herself under Zito's other arm. "Big rock just ahead, Zito," she says. "You'll have to step high."

A guard takes my spot beneath Zito's other arm, and I follow behind, aided by Lupita. As we shuffle back to the castle in the least royal, most awkward procession of my life, I stare at my sister's back. By not involving Khelia's or Isodel's soldiers, she *has* salvaged my plan.

Espiritu is dead. The blight on the land will fade soon enough. And no one will be able to deny that it was the crown princess and her people who made it happen.

II

THE wedding is delayed for two weeks to give Zito and me some time to recover. Within days, the land begins to bloom again, like new growth forest after a cleansing fire. People call it a miracle.

I do not correct them. I haven't decided what to do with my knowledge that the Perditos have allied with Invierne, that magic was used to sicken our land. I say only that Zito and I rescued each other from bandits, that we killed Espiritu and scattered the Perditos. I order my guards to spread the idea that maybe the Perditos were the ones causing God's wrath, that the land heals itself because we chased them away.

When Conde Paxón presents Zito with a new spear—sturdier than his old one and carved with swirling jungle vines—I remember the animagus' broken staff. I'm sure Father Donatzine at the Monastery-at-Amalur would love to study such a talisman. If nothing else, the jewel on the end of it might be of value. But my ankle is too fragile to retrieve it myself, and I'm not sure who to send in my place without raising questions I'm unwilling to answer. I decide to let it go. The jungle will claim it soon enough, with creepers and detritus and thick ferns. It will never be found.

In the days leading to the wedding, Conde Paxón and Lord Jorán share hunting escapades and late-night dessert wines like they've been friends for decades. Soldiers from Khelia and Isodel cheerfully practice together in the yard. Lord Jorán even pulls me aside one day and expresses a sincere hope that Isodel will once again come into the fold of Orovalle, that he is prepared to swear himself as my vassal.

Papá will be proud of everything I have accomplished here.

But Zito says nothing. He refuses to talk about what happened, even to me.

The day of the wedding dawns more beautiful than anyone anticipated. Lady Calla is a lovely bride, and Conde Paxón an endearingly nervous mess. After the ceremony, Zito and I are seated on a dais apart from the others, because of our injuries and my station. He wears a red cloth over his eyes, tied at the back of his head. He leans into his new spear, his ear turned to the sounds of celebration.

"Describe everything to me," he says.

Hope sparks inside me at the genuine interest in his voice. Maybe he's *not* going to sneak away to die on me after all. I swallow hard and say flippantly, "Oh, it's a typical wedding. If you've seen one, you've seen them all. The father of the bride has had too much to drink and dances like an old bear. The groom's men and the bride's maids flirt shamelessly with one another, knowing that on this day, they'll be forgiven anything. The servants linger at the buffet table, sneaking their lord's food while he pretends not to notice."

"And the groom and bride?"

"He is an old, crippled soldier, past his prime, and she is young and beautiful."

Zito's face freezes. After an awkward silence, I hastily add, "They look deliriously happy. It is a marriage of great affection, maybe even love. Still, I give it a fortnight before they are as glum as any married couple."

He doesn't even crack a smile. "And Elisa? How is your sister?"

"She and Lupita are inseparable. I've offered to foster Lupita, you know, when she is old enough. Lady Calla had raptures when I made the suggestion. It's funny—Lupita could have any flowers she wants now that they are blooming, but she chose the scarlet hedge nettle. It looks awful." And wonderful. It really is a good symbol for the people here. Softly, I add, "I have been thinking about Elisa."

Zito says nothing, but he turns his blind face to me.

In a queer twist of fate, my sister is a hero now. The speculation I fed to the guards evolved during the last two weeks. Someone must have wondered if Elisa used the power of her Godstone to chase away the Perditos and heal the land. It's been such a popular notion that none of her protestations can convince them otherwise.

I smile to myself. Elisa will forever have the acclaim for something that Zito and I did. And for some reason, I don't mind at all.

"Thinking what?" Zito prods at last.

"Papá has considered giving Elisa away to one of our lesser but wealthy lords to refill our coffers. But maybe she belongs with someone in a position of *power*. She . . ." For some reason, it's hard to say. But this is Zito. I can say anything to him. "She has potential, Zito. She will act when forced. And when she sets her mind to something . . . Well, getting her away and on her own might be just what she needs."

His features shift slightly, but without his eyes to measure his mood, I'm not sure what it means. I suppose I must get to know my steward all over again. If he stays with me long enough.

"I'm glad you've come to see some worth in her," he says at last. "The two of you, working together, would be a pair to be reckoned with."

He might be right, but I shrug my usual dismissal—a gesture that I realize, belatedly, is wasted on him. So it is his blindness that forces me to say, for once, what is in my heart. "I am willing to work toward that end, Zito, if you promise me that you will be here for it."

And it is like the sun breaking through the clouds to see my friend's lips lift into a tiny smile. "I promise."

THE SHATTERED MOUNTAIN

MARA wakes in the predawn chill. She did not stoke the fire in her tiny bedroom the night before, knowing the cold would rouse her early. She will need the darkness and solitude for her deception.

She swings her legs over the cot and places bare feet on the earthen floor. The chill creeps through the soles of her feet, into her legs, as she fumbles across the tree stump she uses as a nightstand for flint, steel, and tinder.

A spark, a wisp of smoke. She touches a candle wick to the tinder, and the sudden glow makes her feel warmer than she actually is. Or maybe it's just the thought of escape.

She places the candle on the floor so she can find stockings and boots, and the light flickers across her toes. Even more than the candle, more than the thought of getting away, a memory wraps her with warmth and light and love—Julio's fingers tracing her toes with callused but gentle fingers, almost but not quite tickling. She always thought her toes too long and thin to accommodate her too-long, too-thin body. But thinking about Julio makes her wonder if her toes might be a little bit beautiful, too.

From the common room come the rustling of parchment and the clink of a mug set upon the table. Mara's blood freezes, even as her heart pounds out the aching rhythm—*No, no, no, not this morning of all mornings.*

Papá is awake.

She could try to bluff her way past him, but not even the prospect of meeting Julio in the meadow makes her brave enough. She should go back to sleep and try again later. Julio will wait for her. He'll worry, but he'll wait.

Heart sinking, Mara starts to pull her feet back under the quilt, but she kicks the candlestick and sends it soaring. It clatters against the wall, snuffing the flame.

Her hand flies to her mouth to stifle a gasp, but it's too late.

"Mara?" comes the gruff voice. "Is that you?"

No help for it now. She shoves her feet into her boots—too dark to find the stockings—saying, "Yes, Pá. I startled awake."

Leaving the boots unlaced, she pads toward the doorway. Her stomach clenches as she pushes aside the doeskin that separates her bedroom from the common area. "Sorry to disturb you," she says, keeping her voice mild.

Papá sits on a large cushion at a low table. Parchment and scrolls are strewn before him, seeming to writhe in red-orange shadows cast by a flickering candelabra. He stares at her, quill poised in the air, black ink marring his gray beard. The candlelight shades his eyes and his cheekbones; for a moment he looks as gaunt and alien and cruel as an animagus, one of the enemy sorcerers that have been prowling their hills in recent months.

The irony of this comparison is not lost on her.

"I rarely see you up at this hour," she says, trying to sound offhand as she strides toward the adobe hearth. Their *huta* is the largest in the village, with four rooms and a common area large enough for many guests. Her father is the village priest, after all, and very nearly wealthy.

"I'm holding services tomorrow," he says. "With the Inviernos coming closer and closer every day, and the king unwilling to send troops, our people need a call to hope and faith."

As if hope and faith could stop the weapons and sorcery of the Inviernos. "So this will be an important sermon, then?" she says, just to fill the cold air with something besides her own dread. She swings the iron arm holding the kettle over the fire to reheat the water. It squeals; if this were not her last morning in the *huta*, she would oil the joint.

"The most important I have ever given," he says with gravitas and conviction that make her squirm with guilt. He is a good man in so many ways, a devoted shepherd to his flock of people. For the thousandth time, she wishes his kindness extended to her.

If he was up all night working on his sermon, he must sleep soon. Which gives her an idea.

"Would you like some tea, Pá?" Just the tiniest amount of duerma leaf would do it. He's already exhausted. And Mara is the best cook in the village—she can disguise or enhance any flavor. He would never know.

"Yes, thank you."

His quill *scritch-scritch*es against parchment as she sorts through the shelves, gathering herbs for her cheesecloth. Hopefully, she is now forgotten, invisible. Carefully, surreptitiously, she reaches behind a bundle of dried mint for the packet of duerma leaf.

"Are you tending the sheep again today?" he asks, louder this time, and she almost drops it. *Of course* she is tending the sheep. He only asks to remind her how much he hates letting her out of his sight, out of his control.

"Yes," she says, not turning to face him.

"You're not meeting that boy again, are you?"

"Of course not," she lies.

She doesn't hear him move, but suddenly her forearm is in an iron grip. His thumb presses into the flesh above her wrist so hard that tears spring to her eyes. But she knows better than to gasp or wince. Or drop the duerma leaf. Mara blinks rapidly to clear her eyes, then turns to face her father.

His smile is too brittle to fool anyone save by the most meager candlelight. "Is that why you're up so early, Mara?" he says, almost crooning. "Because you can't resist the desires of the flesh?"

She straightens and holds her head high. She shouldn't, because she's taller than he is now, and feeling small makes him mean. But she does it anyway. "I startled awake," she says softly. "But since I did, I might as well head to the meadow early. I spotted a stand of sage yesterday, so I'm bringing my spice satchel. I could gather enough to keep us in savory scones until spring. If you'd rather I didn't go, just say the word."

The only thing Papá enjoys more than sermonizing from the *Scriptura Sancta* is the money she earns at the market with her baking. She has trapped him neatly.

"I don't like you going alone," he murmurs. "It's not safe."

He's right. It's not. Which is why she and Julio must make their escape before the Inviernos have blocked all the roads. But she doubts her safety is his true concern. "Come with me," she coaxes.

His thumb digs so deep that it takes all her control not to cry out, and for a terrifying moment, Mara fears he'll call her bluff.

All at once he releases her. Warm blood rushes into her hand, and she stumbles backward, hitting the shelves.

"Add a few pine needles to the tea," he says, settling back down on his cushion. "I need something tart to keep me awake a while longer."

"Yes, Pá," she says, still clutching the duerma leaf.

2

IT takes almost an hour for Papá to collapse onto the table. She nudges his shoulder gently, but he does not stir. He will know at once what she has done when he does finally wake. Mara will be long gone by then.

She gathers her bow and quiver, her spice satchel and water skin, and leaves through the back door. A dry wash runs behind their *huta*. It's overgrown with yucca and mesquite this time of year, perfect for making a quick escape from the village. Not that anyone would question seeing her on her way to the sheep pens at this hour, but she can't lose the niggling worry that Papá will wake up after all. She imagines him barreling out the door toward her, fist raised to strike.

But the day is so beautiful, and the sheep bleat with such delight at seeing her, that the worry fades as she herds them up the mountain. Mara has always loved early mornings—the clarity of the air, the chirping rock wrens, the waking lizards, the freedom and solitude. She especially loves the way light edges the teeth of the Sierra Sangre, reminding her that not even the mighty mountains can hold back the dawn.

Her bow doubles as a walking staff; it clicks against the rocky trail as she guides them between red-orange buttes and through a gully wash. A quiver of arrows slung across her back rattles with each stride. She's been practicing ever since her father gave her the bow. Last week she bagged two rabbits, and yesterday she scared off a coyote that had prowled too close. But she wouldn't want to test her amateur skill against an Invierno.

Still, growing the flock is the smartest thing she's done in her seventeen years, because duty forces her to leave the village—and her father—almost every day to graze them. Unfortunately, the surrounding area will soon be grazed out, and they'll have to move farther afield. Her father will never allow it, especially now that the foothills are lousy with enemy scouts.

After today, though, it will no longer be her problem. "I'm sorry I have to leave you," she whispers. Her sheep are the one thing about this life she'll miss. They are too relentlessly stupid and sweet to hurt her on purpose.

Her path opens into a drying meadow surrounded by swirling sandstone outcroppings, edged in thirsty cottonwoods. A seasonal creek bed, barely trickling with last week's fall storm, winds through the grass. One of the younger ewes leaps into the air, tail spinning, and takes off across the meadow in an exuberant gallop. Mara understands how she feels.

Her breath catches when arms snake around her waist and a warm body presses against her back. Julio's lips nuzzle her neck. He whispers, "Good morning."

She spins in his arms, pulls his head down, and presses her lips to his. She kisses him deeply, hungrily, until he breaks away, laughing.

But he sobers when he sees her face. The skin around his eyes is prematurely crinkled from days spent on the trap lines, or maybe from too much smiling. It's one of the things she likes best about his face. He scans her from top to bottom. "Did he hurt you?"

Mara looks down, her bruised forearm suddenly screaming with pain.

"Every time he hurts you, I want to kill him," he says. "It's wrong of me, but I can't help it."

It makes her stomach turn to think that Julio might be capable of the same rage as her father. She releases his hands, hides her arms behind her back. "I put a bit of duerma leaf in his tea. He should sleep all afternoon."

His eyes dance. "You didn't!"

It never would have occurred to Mara to be amused were it not for him, and she finds herself smiling back. "I did."

"I hope he wakes with a massive headache."

She glances around the meadow. Julio's pack of supplies is propped up against a cottonwood. "Where is Adán?" she asks. Julio's little brother has been their co-conspirator. Today is his turn to check the trap line, but he agreed to ditch his duties and instead bring his horse for them. After they leave, Adán will herd the sheep back to safety.

Julio rolls his eyes. "Mamá caught him stealing pomegranate

jelly from the cellar. She's making him muck out stalls this morning. He'll be here soon enough."

Mara nods, relieved. Julio's mother won't keep Adán long. His parents are aware of their plan, or at the very least suspect something. For Deliverance Day this year, they gave Julio a brand-new traveling cloak lined with fur. Julio said that when they draped it over him to gauge the fit, his father wrapped him in his arms and held him long enough for Julio to feel awkward.

What must it be like to have loving parents, who encourage you to follow your dreams, even when they don't exactly approve? Even when they might be dangerous?

"I'm worried about the Inviernos," Mara admits. "A man who bought scones from me the other day said they're harassing traders along the northern road now. What if the way west is blocked?"

Julio plunks onto the ground and crosses his legs. He sifts through the grass with his fingers, saying, "Then we join the rebellion."

She snorts. "The rebellion. What a sorry bunch of—"

"What's the king doing to protect us? Nothing! If it weren't for the rebels—"

"You shouldn't say such things so loud!" She sinks to the ground beside him.

Julio yanks a blade of grass and starts chewing on it. "Yes, the sheep might declare me seditious." More seriously, he adds, "Whatever we do, it's only for a year. Once we're married—and your Pá has cooled off—we'll be back."

Papá's temper never cools. It only simmers, hidden, until an explosion brings it to the surface. But it would be cruel to ask Julio to leave his family forever, so instead of protesting, she sprawls out and lays her head in his lap. "So," she says, gazing up at the brightening sky, "we go west as planned, but if the way is blocked, we join the rebellion." She silently considers that her hostile feelings toward the rebellion might have more to do with Belén, the boy who wooed her, then ignored her, then left to join the rebels. "I suppose even sedition is better than asking my father for permission to marry."

"Frankly, I can't decide which is more fraught with adventure and peril."

She laughs giddily, thinking, *Oh, Pá, you are so wrong. It's not the desires of the flesh I can't resist. It's this. The sharing of dreams. The* hope.

His fingers trace her cheek, her neck, her collarbone. She closes her eyes, wanting to savor every sensation, treasuring them up in her memory box so she can take them out for admiring later.

But then her eyes fly open. "I smell smoke. Not a cook fire."

His fingers freeze. "You're sure?"

The scent is off. Not green wood, not firewood. More like rushes, or maybe wool. "My cook's nose is never wrong." She sits up and scans the horizon.

"Stay here." He launches to his feet and dashes toward the nearest outcropping. Despite the dread curling in her throat, she can't help but admire the way he scrambles up the rock, the strong hands that have learned every bit of her body clutching handholds with swift assuredness as he pulls himself to the peak.

He gazes off in the direction of the village, and his mouth drops open in horror.

Julio scrambles back down—more falling than climbing in his rush, and she's shaking her head against what he'll say long before he reaches her.

"The village," he pants. "Burning. All of it."

"The Inviernos," she whispers.

He cups her face in his hands. "We could run," he says.

Hope sparks in her gut, so shining and sharp that it hurts. But she stuffs it away.

"No. My Pá. Your little brother . . ."

"Adán!" he gasps, his face frozen with guilty shock. "How could I not think . . . he could be trapped in the stable!" And then he's off running.

"Oh, God," she whispers at his back. "The duerma leaf."

Mara sprints after him.

3

THEY slow as they approach, fearful of stumbling upon the enemy. The village lies in a small canyon at the base of a mountain. It's usually impossible to see until one is at the edge of the ridge, looking down at it. But today its existence is brutally marked by a beacon of brown-black smoke choking the sky.

They hear the Invierno before they see him—his anklet of bones rattling, the *thwack* of a longbow releasing its arrow, the victory yell. Mara barely holds in a whimper. The Inviernos are up here on the ridge, shooting the people she grew up with like they're sheep penned for slaughter.

They crouch behind a manzanita bush. Julio slides a knife from his boot. He pantomimes creeping through the scrub and taking the Invierno by surprise. She shakes her head in protest, but he grabs her hand, brings her knuckles to his lips. His eyes are dark with intensity, and she hopes he's not saying good-bye.

He's on his feet in a swift, silent movement, and he disappears into the scrub brush.

Mara claws the dirt as fury washes over her. She will not let Julio die. Or young Adán. Or even her papá. She *won't.*

She reaches behind her back and quietly slides an arrow from her quiver.

Mara steps forward in a half crouch even as she notches the arrow against her bowstring. With luck and no wind, she can hit a rabbit at fifteen paces. Can she kill a human at five?

Julio is nowhere to be seen, but the back of the Invierno's head is barely visible through the high scrub. Never has she seen such hair—pale yellow-brown, like aged oak. As she creeps toward him, his longbow comes up. He pulls an arrow, draws, sights something—or someone—in the village below.

Mara abandons stealth. The underbrush stabs her ribs, slices her face as she charges through, yelling. His shot flies wide, and he whirls to face her.

She breaks through the manzanita as he pulls a dagger. She draws her bow. *Focus, breathe.* He lunges, and his eyes—blue as the spring sky—are so startling that her elbow shakes as she lets fly.

The arrow grazes his shoulder with enough impact to twist him around. He rights himself and stumbles toward her. She pulls another arrow from her quiver, tries to notch it, misses, tries again. He is nearly upon her.

He freezes, back arched, eyes wide. Mara sidesteps as he topples forward to reveal Julio standing behind him, holding the blood-soaked skinning knife.

"Are you all right?" he says.

She nods. Her heart races, her hands shake, and something

wet and warm slips down her cheek, but she feels neither pain nor exhaustion. That happens sometimes, when her father raises a hand to her. It might be hours before she understands whether or not she is hurt.

She steps over the body of the Invierno, trying to ignore how human it looks, and together they look down into the burning village.

The blacksmith's stall has burned to the ground, with the attached stable soon to follow. Horses neigh in panic. Villagers scurry everywhere. Most try to flee, but volleys of arrows from the south ridge keep them penned toward the center. Papá's *huta* is intact for now, but it's only a matter of time before the roof catches.

Her breath hitches. The dry wash behind their *huta*! It's overgrown, invisible to outsiders. It hasn't caught fire yet, and she doesn't see any arrows coming from the ridge above it.

Her people could use it to escape, if someone showed them the way.

"Do you see Adán?" Julio says, panic edging his voice.

"Maybe he got away." The lie feels heavy on her tongue.

Julio starts forward. "I have to find—"

Mara grabs his arm. "Look. The east ridge." She points to the tall figure silhouetted against the sky—one of the dreaded animagi. Wind whips his robes taut against his gaunt body and sends his eerie white hair streaming behind him.

He lifts his hand. Something dangles from it, something that shimmers in the morning light. A white-hot firebolt spews from the shimmering thing and explodes against a nearby rooftop. The roof collapses, shooting flames and smoke into the sky.

Mara lurches back, her heel skidding in gravel, as Julio whispers, "Oh, my God."

Her heart hammers with fear and rage. "If I were a little closer, I could shoot him."

"If you miss your first shot, you're dead. I can try with my sling."

"A sling is even more useless long range!"

"We have to do *something*."

Julio pulls her down, out of sight, and Mara is struck breathless by how stupid they were to stand there gaping, right out in the open.

"No one will get out of the village unless the Inviernos are distracted," Julio says.

"The gully behind my father's *huta* is still clear, but probably not for long. If you . . ." She swallows hard against what she is about to suggest. "If you distract them, attack the animagus from behind, I can get them out. I can show them the way."

"It's not just the animagus we have to worry about!"

"It's smoky, and most of the archers are concentrated on the south ridge." She reaches up and cups his cheek. "I'll find your little brother."

The knob of his throat bobs as he swallows. "I'll just have to make a big enough distraction."

"We'll meet afterward."

"Where?"

"The meadow. No, wait." They would be going from one

sheep pen into another. "The cave. Where we first . . ." Tears prick at her eyes. Where they first made love.

He's shaking his head. "That's halfway up the Shattermount!"

"It's safe. Invisible from the outside. We could see anyone coming."

Something crashes below. Smoke billows into the sky.

"Julio, there's no more time! We have to—"

He takes her face in his hands, kisses her once, hard. "I love you, Mara." And he melts into the brush.

4

MARA slips down the gravelly slope. The manzanita tears at her skin and clothes, but it also hides her descent. The smoke is thicker here. Not much time before she won't be able to breathe.

She lands on the valley floor between the stables and the tanner's *huta* and pauses. Adán first, because she promised. Then Papá.

Mara creeps down the alley until she reaches the front of the buildings. Before she can think, before she can be afraid, she bursts from cover and sprints across the plaza, past the stone well, into the market. An arrow zings by her ear, but she keeps pumping arms and legs as fast as she can. She scoots behind a burning market stall. It won't provide a real barrier, but the smoke and flames might make her hard to spot from the ridge.

Gasping for breath, she peers through the gloom. There must be survivors . There *must* be.

Movement, just to her left. A shape materializes. "Mara!"

"Reynaldo!" A boy from one of the surrounding farmsteads.

She has never been so glad to see anyone in her life. Ash-gray tears streak the boy's face.

"Have you seen Adán?"

The market stall behind her collapses on itself. She darts forward, into the cover of smoke, grabbing the boy's arm. Her lungs sting and grit fills her eyes.

"This way," he says, but the smoke is too much. The *hutas* are thickest here, and all of them burn. She pulls him to the ground, where the air is a little clearer, and together they crawl forward through an alley.

More shapes ahead. Children. Huddled on the ground, clutching one another in the lee of the cliff wall. Out of range and sight of the Inviernos, but they will burn soon enough. If they don't suffocate first.

Mara scrambles toward them. There are five, all different ages, and she almost sobs with relief to see Adán. He and Reynaldo are the oldest, almost young men. Adán holds the littlest in his lap, a tiny girl of three or four.

"I know how to escape," Mara says without preamble. "There's a gully behind my papá's house. We can use it to sneak out."

Adán hitches the little girl to his chest. "They'll shoot us!" he says.

"Better than burning alive," Reynaldo counters.

Mara meets Adán's gaze. "Julio is providing a distraction. We'll go carefully, try to stay out of sight, but we have to do it now."

The children exchange terrified glances. "Now!" Mara yells.

"On your feet or I will thrash you!" She's not above threats if it means saving lives.

They all jump to their feet.

"Crouch low to avoid smoke. Put up your shirts, like this." She lifts the collar of her blouse over her mouth and nose, and they copy her, eyes wide with hope and fear. "Follow close, and don't look back. Reynaldo, can you take up the rear? Make sure no one straggles."

They set off, and Mara moves as fast as she dares. She keeps between the back walls of the *hutas* and the looming cliff face. It provides the best cover from shooters on the ridge, but the smoke huddles here, and within moments most of the children are coughing.

A smoking pile of rubble marks the end of the *hutas*, and Adán lets a small sob escape. It's Julio's family home.

Mara grabs the hand of the nearest child, to absorb comfort as much as to give it, and says to them all, "We wait for a break in the arrows, then we run, as fast as we can, to my father's house. Understood?"

Their sooty faces bob up and down.

"Reynaldo, are you strong enough to carry the little one?" She'd do it herself, but she might need her hands free for her bow.

"I . . . yes."

"Good. Wait for my signal." She peers out of the smoke, into the clearer plaza. Large blackened lumps pepper the paver stones. They steam and smoke, and bright red peeks through cracks in their charred surfaces. Maybe, with all the smoke and the chaos, the children won't recognize them for bodies.

Arrows rain down toward the smithy. Is someone trapped there?

Shouts sound from the ridge, and the arrows cease to fall. *Thank you, Julio.*

"Now!" she shouts, and the children burst from cover into the plaza. Adán leads, and Mara yearns to sprint after him, but she takes up the rear, yelling, "Go, go, go, almost there!"

Her father's *huta* is in decent shape compared to the others; only the back wall burns. But that means the fire will soon spread to the gully.

Mara guides them around it to the gravelly slope. "Everyone, into the ditch. It's steep—grab the bushes as you slide down . . . that's it."

The tiny girl is the last of the children to go down. Mara lifts her and lowers her into Reynaldo's waiting arms.

"Keep your heads down," Mara orders. "Follow the gully until you reach the stand of cottonwoods. Hide there. If the Inviernos come, run. If I'm not back by the time the sun touches the earth, run."

"You're not coming?" Adán says, his voice coarse with coughing.

"I need to find my pá. And any other survivors. I'll be back as soon as I can."

"Maybe you can find my sister," a boy says.

"And Mamá," says a girl of about ten. "She made me go, and then the roof . . ."

"Muffin, my goat," says the tiny girl.

Oh, God. She can't possibly save them all. "I'll do my best," Mara says. "Now go! Be brave, be smart. Reynaldo is in charge until I get back." And she steps away before she can change her mind or hear any more about lost loved ones.

Mara enters Papá's *huta*. Smoke fills the common room; she can barely see an arm's length in front of her. "Papá? Are you here?" A dagger of guilt twists in her chest. If he's dead, it's her fault. "Papá?"

She shuffles around blindly, feeling with feet and hands. Her shins knock the table, and she works around it, searching for a body. She doubles over with coughing. Her lungs are on fire, and dizziness wavers her vision. She drops to the floor and breathes deep of the clearer air before moving forward on hands and knees.

Mara finds the settee that her father loves to offer to guests, the prayer table where he burns candles to God, the shelf where he keeps his manuscripts. She does a complete circle of the room, ending up at the kitchen area—but there is no sign of Papá.

At the edge of the hearth is her father's travel bag, the one he uses when he leaves the village to do God's work.

Supplies. They left Julio's pack in the meadow, but they'll need something to get them to the next village.

It is a good thing she has practiced sneaking out during so many dark mornings, because she can find everything she needs, even sightless. She grabs the tinderbox, her favorite skinning knife, a cooking pot, a round of cheese, a package of deer jerky, last night's bread loaf, a small pot of honey, a half-empty flour sack, an extra quiver of precious arrows.

Her father's bag barely holds everything. Despair almost consumes her right then. She has enough to feed five children for only a day. Two if they ration. But the nearest village is almost a week away.

Maybe they can supplement their food on the way. She'll assign the littlest ones to watch out for certain plants as they go. They'll make it somehow, even though Mara is not a very good hunter.

Papá presented the bow to her as a Deliverance Day gift, as a show of wealth more than anything. *See? My daughter doesn't use a sling like the rest of you. Only a pine bow will do.* She took it up only because it was an efficient way to scare predators from her sheep, not because she expected to hunt regularly.

The sheep! Her sweet, stupid sheep. Abandoned in the meadow without a moment's hesitation.

She slips the bag's strap over her shoulder. "Papá? Where are you? We need to—"

Something crashes into her back, knocking her to the floor. A huge weight pins her down, and she fights to breathe.

"You wicked girl!" her father rages. A fist crashes into her shoulder blade. "You brought this down upon us! With your sin. And now you *steal* from me? Before leaving me to die?"

She squirms out from beneath him, but he catches her ankle. "No, Pá! I came back to find you. I was worried—"

He reaches for her face, misses, grabs a chunk of hair instead, ripping it from her scalp.

Blackness edges her vision. She knows what will happen

next. Her mind will go away. To a place where there is no pain, where she can watch, detached, as he pummels her.

Not this time. The children need her. She claws her way back from the edge of consciousness, to where grit from the floor grinds into her raw, damaged scalp and unrelenting fingers dig into her lower leg. She tries to yank her ankle away, but his grip is firm.

Terror builds inside her, becomes fury, becomes strength. She channels it all into a single, tremendous kick to Papá's face.

He releases her ankle.

She scrambles back toward him. "Pá? Papá?" She shakes his limp body. "We have to go! Please . . ."

Blood oozes from his nose, soaks his beard. Did she kill him? She reaches for his neck to check his pulse, but the back wall of the *huta* collapses. Sparks shoot into the gully where the children are fleeing.

Mara grabs the travel bag and darts outside, leaving her father behind.

5

SHE pauses at the edge, about to plunge into the gully, but movement catches her eye. There, by the smithy. A dark shape in the smoke.

Mara can't tell if it's a person or a horse, but either one is worth the risk. She dashes toward it. Arrows rain down around her, and her greatest fear roils in her heart like a black cloud. If the Inviernos are shooting again, it means Julio no longer distracts them.

She plunges into the cover of smoke, choking and coughing. "Hello!" she calls. "Anyone here?"

"Here," comes a tiny voice.

She drops to her knees and crawls toward it. It's Carella, the smith's wife. She huddles against the stall, clutching her small daughter in her lap.

"Barto is dead," the woman moans. "Dead, dead, dead."

Mara should feel sympathy, but all she can muster is panic. "On your feet, woman! Or your child dies too."

Carella blinks up at her. Tears streak her ash-dusted face.

"There's a group of survivors waiting for us," Mara says. "We're making a run to the next village."

Carella whimpers, clutching tighter to her daughter.

Mara slaps the woman across the face, but then she chokes out a sob, shocked at herself.

But Carella is getting to her feet. "Which way?" she says wearily, then doubles over with coughing.

"Let me," Mara says, grabbing the child from Carella's arms. The girl is about five or six, too big to carry easily, but her mother's movements are slow and staggered, as if she's badly injured. Or maybe she has breathed too much smoke.

Carella steps from the cover of the smithy into the plaza.

"Wait!" Mara calls. "This way; we must stick to cover."

Carella looks over her shoulder. "Take her. Keep her safe." She hobbles forward, into the light, clear air, revealing the blood soaking the back of her skirt, streaming down her right ankle. She reaches her arms to the sky as if summoning heaven itself. "Go, Mara! Now!"

Mara freezes.

A firebolt streams through the sky and plunges into Carella's torso. She stumbles but does not fall, even as her blouse and hair catch flame, turning her into a fiery goddess. "Go!" she screams.

A second firebolt sends her crashing to the ground.

Mara hitches the child tight to her chest and flees.

6

THE children are waiting right where she told them to. The tiniest girl's chin and blouse are soaked with red-tinged phlegm. At Mara's questioning look, Reynaldo says, "She's been coughing up blood."

Oh, God. If she has internal injuries, there is nothing they can do.

Reynaldo's eyes flash when he notices Mara's patchy hair and her bruised eye—her bruised eye . . . when did that happen?—but his gaze slides over it like water, a veil clouds his face, and her injuries are suddenly invisible to him. She's seen it happen dozens of times before. The villagers always turned a blind eye to this, the handiwork of her father.

"We need to get away," Mara says. She doesn't want to scare the children more than necessary, but she can't bring herself to lie either. "The gully behind me is starting to catch fire, and the Inviernos could have scouts in the area. So we move fast and quietly. There will be no talking unless it's to call out a warning. Understood?"

They nod in unison.

"What about my brother?" Adán asks. "Did you see Julio?"

"He'll meet us on the Shattermount."

As they exchange fearful glances and murmur among themselves, Mara considers that lying might have been better after all.

"Mamá says I'm not allowed on the Shattermount," says one little girl.

The boy beside her nods solemnly. "There are bears."

"Flash floods!" says Adán.

Mara sighs, knowing there is no safe way to lead them. "Yes, there might be bears. And flash floods. And even ghosts," she says. "But do you know what the Shattermount doesn't have?"

The children shake their heads.

"It doesn't have Inviernos. It's too frightening a place for them. Only Joyans are brave enough for the Shattermount."

"I'm not afraid," says Adán. A chorus of "Me neither" follows.

Thank you, Adán.

"Will we climb the slope or stick to the fault?" Reynaldo asks.

"The fault. It's out of sight." Julio's family maintained a trap line on the Shattermount, as did a few other villagers. No one has seen signs of Inviernos there. Yet. But it's better to be cautious. No one had seen them in the village either, before this morning. "We'll keep an eye on the sky." Rain, even a day's journey away, could mean a flash flood.

Reynaldo nods agreement, and she suddenly wants to hug his gangly form, just for being almost grown up, someone who can help make decisions and look out for the little ones.

They set off, quietly as promised. They walk for hours, and Mara's thighs burn with effort, for the Shattermount is a steep, wide-based monolith that marks the transition from desert foothills to the mighty slopes of the Sierra Sangre. In its upper reaches, the desert scrub gives way to pine, the gravel to granite, the rain to snow. A thousand years ago, or maybe more, a great cataclysm opened a huge fault line right down the center. This shattering resulted in a mountain with a deep groove and twin peaks. Julio always compared them to the horns of a mighty goat. Mara preferred to think of them as the ears of a great lynx.

The sun is low at their backs, sweat is stinging Mara's ruined scalp, and a few of the children are beginning to stumble from exhaustion when they walk right into a campsite.

The children rush forward, recognizing a few friends. Four more survivors—three children and one badly injured adult. Two horses. A pack full of supplies. A cheery fire sending smoke tendrils into the sky.

Mara sizes it up quickly, but as everyone hugs and cries and laughs with delight, she hangs back, her relief at seeing others turning to despair. Because she made a mistake, one that could have gotten them killed. She should have scouted ahead. What if this had been an Invierno camp?

No more mistakes. She strides over to the campfire and kicks dirt and gravel onto it. When the flames are low enough, she stomps it out.

"What are you doing?" asks a young boy, his face furious.

She whirls on him. "Have you lost your mind? Do you want to bring the Inviernos down on us? You might as well send them a letter. 'Here we are! Survivors for you to come kill!' I can't believe you all were so stupid." Her face reddens as the words leave her mouth.

Joy dissipates from the camp like a drop of water poured on scorched earth. Some stare guiltily at her. Others glare.

With a resigned voice, Reynaldo says, "Mara's right. No fires. Not until it's safe."

Mara knows she should say something encouraging. Something optimistic. But she doesn't know what. She has never been good with people. A bit withdrawn, Julio tells her. Due to a lifetime of hiding her bruises and scars—the ones on her body and on her soul.

She looks to the one adult in the group for support. He sits slumped over by the now-dead fire, clutching his side. He raises his head briefly, and she finally recognizes him—it's Marón, owner of the Cranky Camel and the richest man in the village. His skin is corpse-white, his eyes glazed. The two horses belong to him. With a start, she realizes that he didn't lead the children here. He is too far gone. *They* rescued *him*.

And suddenly Mara knows what to say.

"You are all very brave for making it this far, and I'm proud of you."

7

THERE are not enough blankets to stave off the cold night.
Mara and Reynaldo organize the children into groups and tell
them to huddle close for sleep. "We'll have a fire when we get
to the cave," Mara promises them.

Mara lies down, with Carella's daughter and the tiny coughing girl tucked into the crook of her curved body. And when
bright morning sun batters her eyelids awake, she is surprised
to find that she slept long and hard.

But Marón, the tavern owner, died during the night. Mara
enlists Adán's help to drag his stiffening body into the brush
and cover it with deadfall—quickly, before all the children
wake. When they do, she tells them the truth. One little girl
collapses to the ground, crying. His daughter.

As they break camp and prepare for the day's journey, she
overhears them talking about loved ones. So many friends and
family members that they left behind. Some are known to be
dead. But most were simply separated sometime during the
chaos of the attack. Most, they hope, might still be alive.

But Mara saw too many bodies, blackened and oozing, for there to be many survivors. And suddenly she wonders if she should have let the children see Marón's body. Maybe a large, single dose of pain now is better than the slow, burning pain of withering hope. Maybe seeing death up close is an important part of saying good-bye.

Right before they set off, Mara takes stock of their provisions. In addition to the supplies in Pá's bag, Reynaldo and two others thought to grab jerky and water skins. The pack on Marón's horse holds cooking utensils, a bag of dates, two blankets, a knife, a spongy onion, and a round of bread. It's so much better than nothing, but they'll need to find food fast. The nearest village is a week's journey, but Mara isn't sure it's the safe choice. It might suffer the same fate as her own village. Maybe when they get close, she and Reynaldo can scout ahead.

But first, the cave—and Julio. *Please be all right, Julio. Please be safe.* She has purposely not allowed herself to consider the way the rain of arrows started again just as suddenly as it stopped. As if the distraction Julio provided had vanished like smoke.

They hike all day to reach the cave. The climb is steep, and the little ones tire quickly. She and Julio reached it in half that time, on that precious, precious day months ago.

It's exactly the way she remembered, with a sun-soaked ledge outside the crooked opening. The air is drenched with a clean, sharp scent from the juniper surrounding the ledge, keeping the cave invisible from below. What she *doesn't* see is any sign of life. No campfire. No footprints. No Julio.

She helps the tiny, coughing girl onto the ledge, then Mara abandons the children to rush inside the cave. "Julio?" she calls, and her voice echoes back with emptiness. "Julio?" she repeats, as if calling louder will summon him.

Someone comes to stand beside her. "He's not here, is he?" Adán says.

"He will come," Mara says, though her gut twists. She takes a deep breath. "All right, everyone. Let's get settled. Reynaldo, if you build that fire, I'll make a soup tonight."

The cavern already boasts a fire pit in its center. It's a narrow but long chamber, with a ceiling high enough that only she and Reynaldo must hunch over. She knows from experience that cracks in the ceiling provide an outlet for smoke. There is plenty of room for all nine of them during the day, but a shortage of level floor space will make sleeping a challenge. There might be space for everyone if she, Adán, and Reynaldo sleep outside on the ledge, rotating watches.

Mara throws together a thin soup of jerky with onions and garlic. As they take turns spooning it from her cooking pot, she sizes up the group. She is the oldest, at seventeen. Reynaldo is fifteen, Adán fourteen. Everyone else is younger, down to the tiny girl, who can't be more than four. Mara is glad to note that her coughing has subsided, and it no longer turns up blood. Maybe something will go right for them after all.

She doesn't know all their names. Her village isn't that large, but skirmishes with the Inviernos have caused a lot of migration among the hill folk, and when the animagus burned her village, it was half full of strangers.

She could ask their names. She *should* ask their names. But she's suddenly overcome with the sense that she might learn who they are only to see them die.

Later. She'll ask later. She wants to be silent and alone with her thoughts a little bit longer.

Looking into their ash-covered faces, their eyes filled with both hope and terror, Mara marvels at how two such opposite-seeming emotions can exist inside her. She wants to save them. But bitterness grinds away at her heart too. These are the children of the people who turned blind eyes to her pain. They bought her pastries and her wool quick enough, but never in her life did anyone ask, "Mara, how are you *really?*" Until Julio.

Once Julio arrives, she won't have to be in charge anymore. He'll be the oldest of their group, at nineteen. He's confident and outgoing, well liked by everyone. He'll know how to deal with the children. Julio likes taking care of people. He'll relish the responsibility.

Mara is about to go out to the ledge to take the first watch, but the tiny girl toddles over. Mara sits as still as a statue as the girl climbs into her lap. She grabs a fistful of Mara's shirt and snuggles in tight. Then Carella's daughter sidles up, lays her head on Mara's thigh, and falls fast asleep.

After a moment, Mara's shoulders relax. She wraps one arm around the tiny girl and lets her other hand rest on Carella's daughter's silky head.

8

THE next morning, Julio still has not come. Adán stands on the ledge, gazing down the mountain. He is a lot like his brother—the same long limbs, the same straight black hair bleached red at the temples. His hands are as big as paddles, hinting that he might be even taller than Julio someday.

Mara steps up beside him, squinting against the morning sun.

"He's coming, right, Mara?" Adán says.

"He's coming."

"And *then* what are we going to do?"

She shrugs. "Julio will know. He'll probably lead us to the nearest village. Some of these children might have family there."

"I'm not sure that's a good idea," says a voice at her back, and she turns.

Reynaldo's curly hair is sleep mussed, and his wide-spaced eyes blink against the sun. Mara has always thought him young looking for his age, with his round cheeks and open gaze. But there is something old and weary about him now. Perhaps they've all aged years in the last day.

"What do you mean?" Mara probes.

"Our village isn't the only thing that burned."

As he stares out into the empty expanse of sky, something in his face prompts Mara to say, "Your farmstead. Is that why you were in the village yesterday?"

He nods. "They killed everyone. All the livestock. Burned our . . . I ran to the village to warn everyone. But I was too late. And I've seen smoke on the horizon."

Gently, Mara says, "You helped me save these children. You weren't too late for that."

He swallows hard and nods, but he says nothing.

Mara crosses her arms and hugs her shoulders tight. She wishes Marón had lived. He was a smart businessman, and his tavern was a cornerstone of their community. He would have known what to do. "So you think the nearest village suffered the same fate?"

"All of them, Mara. All of them within two weeks' journey. It's war, now. Full out."

Adán whirls on him, tears in his eyes. "We have to go *somewhere*!"

"We don't have enough supplies to stay here forever," Mara agrees. "We hardly have enough to get us through the next two days."

Reynaldo says, "Maybe we could hunt—"

"Game is scarce," Mara interrupts. "The fires will have driven most of it away."

Reynaldo looks down, scuffs the toe of his leather boots against the rock ledge. "I know of a place, but . . ."

Mara and Adán regard him expectantly. "But . . . ?" Mara prompts.

"It's a secret. I'm not supposed to tell."

Mara inhales sharply. "The rebel camp. You know where it is." Julio was always so sure it existed, that the rumors were true. A safe, hidden place, somewhere west of here in the scrub desert, where an oasis provides good grazing and even some farming.

Reynaldo says, "My cousins Humberto and Cosmé went there last year. I visited once. They invited me to join, but my Pá needs . . . needed me."

The tiny hope sparking in Mara's heart is all the more precious for how fragile and weak it is. "Would they take us in, do you think? Could you show us the way?"

"I can. But it's on the other side of the Shattermount, where the hills start to become true desert. A week away. We should leave right now. Before our food runs out."

"No!" Adán says.

Mara nods at the boy. "We'll wait for Julio."

Reynaldo sighs. "What if he doesn't come?"

"We'll wait," she repeats.

"But, Mara . . ."

"Two days. Give us two days."

Reynaldo nods once, sharply. "Two days."

9

Two days later, the children are restless and hungry, the shallow, hastily dug latrine is full, and there is no sign of Julio. There is no sign of anyone else, either. Reynaldo and Adán scouted back toward the village to no avail. Mara searched the area around the cave but found only flood-tumbled boulders and dried brush. Though she says soothing words to the children, she has come to believe they are all who remain.

Overlooked, because they were the smallest and most helpless.

Mara goes through the motions of heating up leftover soup, breaking camp, and packing—all without speaking. She will do what she can to get the children to safety, because it is a purpose, something to focus her thoughts on. But after? She doesn't know what comes after.

One little boy tugs on her shirt and asks, "Are we leaving today, Mara?" She can only nod wordlessly. She is an overfilled water skin, her sides stretched too thin from the pressure, and if she opens her mouth everything will come bursting out—grief, rage, despair.

They made their food stretch longer than they anticipated. Adán bagged two jerboas the previous day with his sling, and Mara made a stew of the tiny rodents. She made sure no one was looking when she slipped the hearts, livers, and even the wobbly stomachs into her pot. She made the children wash down their stew with a brisk juniper tea, and everyone went to sleep with full bellies.

Now she worries about water. The trickle running down the Shattermount's giant fault will be dry in a day or so. They need another storm. But a storm on the Shattermount almost invariably means a flood.

"Which way?" Reynaldo asks as they gather on the ledge before setting off. "Do we stick to the ridge or climb down through the ravine?"

The mountain is not lush like its brothers farther east. It is a lone monolith, too near the desert. "We would be exposed on the ridge," Mara says. "Visible to any Inviernos still in the area." And the Inviernos are practiced archers—far more skilled than she is. They come from a place where wood is plentiful, and their beautiful bows are sturdy and tall, meant for long-range. "They wouldn't even have to get close to take us apart."

"If it rains . . ."

"We'll climb out at the first sign."

Reynaldo nods agreement.

They give Adán a head start. Like his older brother, he has spent days in the wilderness, and of all of them is most suited to scouting ahead in stealth. After Mara warns the rest of the group to silence, they set off after him.

They will travel down the fault line, then circle the base of the mountain until they reach the desert side. From there, Reynaldo will guide them through the warren of buttes and fissures that make up the scrub desert to the secret rebel camp. It's a good plan, the best one they have. But Mara plods along by rote, putting one foot in front of the other in numb silence.

She and Reynaldo carry the tiny girl in shifts, and they're about to do a handoff so Mara can navigate a boulder in their path when she hears something.

The cracking of a branch. The rustle of leaves. Coming from behind.

Mara shoves the tiny girl at Reynaldo, swings her bow around her shoulder, reaches back, and draws an arrow from her quiver.

The scuff of a boot. Definitely not a deer or a fox.

Mara notches her arrow. "Get behind me," she whispers, fast and low. "Now!" The children scurry to obey.

She glares at the path they just traveled, trying to parse a face or figure among the dead windfalls and scattered boulders. A manzanita bush waves violently. Mara draws her bow until the fletching rests against her cheek.

A face materializes. Streaked with sweat and blood. Wild-eyed.

"Julio!" She may have screamed it. Mara drops her bow and sprints forward, reaching him just as he topples forward into her arms.

His sudden weight almost drives her to her knees, but she holds firm. His back is sticky and wet, his skin fevered. She drags him to level ground, then gently lays him down, instinctively stretching him out on his stomach.

Sure enough, the broken shaft of an arrow protrudes from his lower back. He gasps, his cheek grinding into the dirt, as she peels back his shirt to expose the wound.

The skin around it is swollen and oozing. The arrowhead is not deep, but it might be lodged in a rib. At least it missed his vital organs. They could have treated it easily two days ago. But infection has set in, and now streaks of sickly black zigzag across his skin.

"Oh, Julio."

"Mara," he whispers. "You shouldn't have waited for me."

If he is clearheaded enough to have made it to their cave, read the signs of recent occupation, and tracked them here, then there is hope for him yet.

Hope. Such a dangerous thing.

She traces his cheek with a forefinger. "I need to get this arrow out," she says.

"I know."

"I'll have to scrape out the infection. It will hurt."

"I know."

The children crowd around. They stare at his oozing wound with a mix of delight and revulsion. "That's gross," says one boy, peering closer.

"I have duerma leaf in my satchel," Mara says. "I can at least make sure you sleep before and after."

Julio murmurs something that she takes to be assent. She bends over and plants a quick kiss on his hot forehead, then leaps to her feet. "Reynaldo, go find Adán. I'll get a fire going to heat up my knife."

"But the fire . . . the smoke . . ."

"We have to get that arrow out."

Reynaldo frowns, then disappears down the ravine.

She floats through her preparations, a grin occasionally turning up the corners of her lips. Julio is alive. Alive, alive, alive. She steals glances at him as she rims a fire pit, gathers firewood, kindles a tiny spark into a bright flame.

Mara heats up the last of their water. She uses a cupful to make a tea of the duerma leaf, which Julio sips slowly from his awkward position on his stomach. She will need the remainder for cleaning the wound.

She doesn't want to let the arrowhead fester inside Julio's body a moment more, but she needs Adán and Reynaldo to hold him down while she works. So she sits by the fire, one hand trailing in Julio's matted hair, the other holding her blade over the flames.

"My brother?" Julio mutters. "Is he . . ."

"Adán is safe. He's scouting ahead. I sent someone to fetch him."

Julio wilts against the ground, as if his body is finally able to let go an excess of air. "Thank you, Mara," he breathes. "God, that's a relief. And your pá? Did you find him?"

Mara can't meet his eyes. "I found him."

"Oh. I'm sorry."

She pokes at a glowing branch with her knife, sending sparks flying. She whispers, "I found him alive."

Julio says nothing. Mara feels his eyes on her as he waits patiently. He could draw secrets from a rock this way, by letting the empty silence stretch on until the rock has no choice but to fill it with words. It's how he got Mara to tell him all the things her pá had done.

Mara doesn't mind. Because Julio—unlike everyone else she has ever known—truly wants to listen.

"He tried to hurt me," she says finally. "Even though I came back to help. He thought I was stealing. I think he was crazed from smoke, maybe from the duerma leaf I gave him. So I kicked at him to get away, and I . . . I think I killed him. Either way, I left him to die." She turns a defiant gaze on him. "I know I should feel guilty. But I don't. Not at all."

She watches carefully as the shock on his face fades to acceptance.

"You're free of him," he says finally.

She nods, unable to speak. Free of *him*, yes. But she doesn't feel free. Maybe when Julio recovers. Maybe then.

With the rustle of dry brush, Adán and Reynaldo return. Adán barrels forward, tears streaming down his face, and drops to his knees beside his brother. He reaches down to hug him, but Mara says, "Easy. Don't jostle the wound."

"Hello, Adán," Julio breathes. Mara hopes it's the duerma-leaf tea making him sound even weaker than before. "I hope you've been keeping an eye on my girl for me?"

Adán nods, swiping at his cheeks with the back of his hand.

"Even though you're too ugly for her."

"True," Julio says. "I hope . . ." His voice devolves into a cough. "I hope she likes scars. This one is going to be huge."

"I love scars," Mara says, but her voice trembles. Coughing is a bad, bad sign.

Her blade glows red. It's now or never.

"We're getting this arrow out. Reynaldo, take his shoulders. Adán, his legs. He'll try to throw you off. He won't be able to help himself. You *must* hold him down. Do you understand?"

"I can help," says Carella's daughter. "I'm a good helper!"

Mara almost snaps at her to go away, but changes her mind. "Could you . . ." She searches her mind for a task to keep the girl busy and out of her way. "Hold his feet? That would be a big help."

The girl nods solemnly. Everyone gets into position.

Reynaldo reaches for a twisted bundle of mesquite and snaps off a large twig. He slides it into Julio's mouth and encourages him to bite down. "Don't want you biting off your own tongue," he says.

Mara hesitates. She has treated all sorts of minor wounds, for their village had no doctor. But she has never removed an arrow. What if she makes it worse? "Everyone ready?" she asks, knife poised.

They nod, eyes wide.

Mara touches the burning knife to Julio's back. He hisses as it sizzles his skin, but he doesn't move. She shoves the blade down alongside the arrow shaft. He screams.

She works fast, abandoning finesse. There is so much pus,

and the flesh is so swollen that it's hard to see. He grunts horribly, over and over like a hungry pig, and his body thrashes around. "Hold him!" Mara yells.

Adán squeezes his eyes tight, and tears leak from them as he strains to hold his brother down.

Mara cuts away dead flesh, sopping up viscous, red-tinged fluid as she goes. Finally she exposes the arrowhead enough to get a grip on it. It's lodged in his rib. *You will not vomit, you will not vomit, you will not vomit.*

She slows down to dig at the bone with the point of her blade. Too much pressure and she'll crack it. Julio yells one last time and goes limp. She breathes relief.

Once the arrowhead is loosened a bit, she wraps her hands around it. Before she can think too hard, she gives it a powerful jerk, and it comes free. Blood pours from the wound.

While her knife reheats in the fire, she cleans the wound as best as she can, using the last of the boiled water. Cleaning helps her see that most of the blood is coming from one tiny spot. So she lays the blade against his flesh and cauterizes it. She gags on the scent. She's not the only one; Reynaldo lurches to the side of the ravine and vomits into the mesquite.

Mara sits back on her heels, wiping sweat from her forehead with a sleeve. "It is done," she says to no one in particular. Her hands are soaked with Julio's blood.

"Aren't you going to stitch it up?" Adán says.

"I'm going to let it drain," she says. "Might help the infection." She's guessing about that. All she has are guesses—that draining the wound is the right thing to do. That Inviernos won't patrol the Shattermount's fault. That there is indeed a secret haven where these children will be safe.

She feels a hand on her shoulder and turns to find Reynaldo standing above her. His face is pale, but he's steady now. "We can't stay here," he says. "Especially with a fire."

Julio shouldn't be moved. Not for days. But Reynaldo is right. Staying in one place will just bring the Inviernos down on top of them. There is also the small matter of provisions. They will use the last of their food tonight. Nothing but a bread round and a handful of dates shared among eleven people will ensure they all wake with aching, empty bellies.

"We'll move at first light," Mara says. "I'll strap him to one of the horses if I have to."

"I'll hunt tonight," Reynaldo says. "Maybe I can turn up a rabbit."

Mara nods. "Just be careful. This mountain might be crawling with Invierno scouts."

10

REYNALDO does not find a rabbit. He does, however, encounter a burned-down farmstead with a cellar. In the cellar, he finds three musty turnips, a jar of pomegranate jelly, a side of bacon, and two frightened boys.

He brings them back to their campsite, and Mara is both delighted and dismayed to see them. Two more survivors. Two more mouths to feed.

The boys themselves, ten and thirteen, are so happy to see everyone that they burst into tears. Mara hugs them tight, even though they might be a bit old for hugging, and assures them that they are safe.

When did she become such a liar?

She gets everyone organized for sleep—small children with older ones, two or three to a blanket—then lies down beside Julio, who still sleeps soundly. She yearns to wrap her arms around him but doesn't dare jostle the wound. She is chilled, her shoulder aches from the hard ground, and her stomach rumbles with hunger, so it is hours before she finally drifts off into restless sleep.

In the morning, her first conscious thought is for Julio. She puts a hand on his shoulder, terrified that she won't feel the rise and fall of his breathing. But she does. It's steady and even. Almost healthy. The tiny spark of hope inside her burns hot and bright.

His eyelids flutter at her touch, and when he opens his eyes and sees her, he smiles.

"How do you feel?" she asks, reaching for his bandages. They are soaked with brownish drainage.

He winces as she peels them back. "I feel wonderful," he says. "Like I could fight the Inviernos, carry Adán over my shoulder, and dance a jig all at the same time."

Her lips twitch. "Well, I'm glad to hear it. Because it turns out we're running away together to join the rebellion after all."

He reaches for her hand and gives it a weak squeeze. "I saw this going differently in my head."

She sighs. "Me too. But . . . as long as we're together, right?"

He frowns. "No."

Something unpleasant curls in her belly. "What do you mean?" she asks carefully.

He lifts his head. "Mara. Love. Don't pin all your hopes on me. You are so much more than that. Instead of saying 'as long as we're together,' I'd much rather you say, 'as long as I'm alive.'"

She squeezes his hand. "I can't imagine life without you. I don't want to."

"I don't want to imagine a life without you either. But I do worry . . . sometimes . . . that you only *think* you love me. That you've had so little kindness in your life that . . ." His voice breaks off at the horror on her face. "Oh, Mara, I'm not saying this well. That damn arrow has addled my mind. . . ."

Mara brushes dark hair away from his forehead. "I do love you. And you know it."

He lets his head fall back to the earth and closes his eyes. "I just need . . . a little more rest."

"Sleep," Mara orders. "I'll rouse you when we're ready to go."

He does not respond, and Mara waits to see him breathe before stepping away.

11

AFTER a quick breakfast of cold bacon, Mara cleans Julio's wound and gives him fresh bandages. Not *clean* bandages, alas. The best she can do is tear a strip from one of the blankets. After letting the wound drain all night, she really should stitch it now. But she has no needle. Tonight, if it has worsened, she'll have to cauterize the whole thing.

With Reynaldo's and Adán's help, she gets Julio on one of the two packhorses. He can barely hold himself up, preferring to drape against the horse's neck. They may have to tie him down soon.

The sun shines bright and warm as they set off, but smoke has diffused into the air, coating the earth with a brownish haze. The thin trickle of water winding through their ravine is nearly dry. It pools in occasional shady puddles, warm and brackish. Mara will let the children drink from the stagnant water as a last resort, but it's bound to make their bellies ache.

After a few hours, the tiny girl says, "I'm hungry."

At least she's no longer coughing.

"Me too," says one of the new boys.

Mara sighs. She knew it was coming. But their food is in such short supply that she can't feed them until they make camp tonight. "Keep an eye out for greens," she orders the children. "Winter cress, aloe, nopales. We might still find some juniper berries. If you get too hungry, you can chew on white-pine needles."

At worst, the task will busy the children enough to keep them from complaining. At best, a few succulents might keep their thirst at bay. Once they leave the mountain to drop into the desert, food will be in even scarcer supply. She decides not to think about that just yet.

They travel in silence. Mara can't remember ever seeing such a silent group of children. There is only the sound of their footfalls displacing pebbles, the *clop-clop* of hooves, the squeal of an occasional raptor. And farther away, hollow and distant, the clap of thunder.

"Stop! Everyone, stop." Mara turns in place, neck craning to view the sky. There is not a cloud to be seen. The storm must be on the desert side of the mountain. If so, it would be a rarity. Something that only happens in late fall.

Of course, it *is* late fall.

The sky cracks again, closer this time.

"That was thunder," Reynaldo says.

"I don't see clouds," says Adán.

"What is it?" calls Julio from his horse. "What's going on?"

Mara eyes the ravine wall. Steep, but climbable. For her, at least. The littler ones might struggle.

"If we climb up to the ridge, anyone can see us," Reynaldo says.

"If we don't, we could be caught in a flood," says Adán.

"Maybe the storm is far away."

"What if it's not?"

Mara looks back and forth between them. They're both right. What should she do? She hates having to be the one to decide.

"We'll go a little farther," she says at last. "Look for a better place to climb up." Julio and the horses might not make it up the side without an easier incline.

Thunder rolls again as she beckons them forward. The air temperature takes a sudden drop; it happens so fast that she looks up at the ridge, half expecting to see an animagus who has wrought the change through magic.

"Everyone look for a place to climb up," she orders. The wind is gaining strength, and she must shout to be heard. She prays there are no enemy scouts nearby.

One of the little boys begins to cry. Carella's daughter sidles over and grabs his hand, and together they wind down the ravine, Mara not far behind.

"The walls are getting steeper," Reynaldo observes.

Her heart sinks. She was hoping that she was imagining it. "Keep moving," she urges.

The wind lifts her hair from her neck, and she looks back toward the mountain peaks. Sure enough, blue-black clouds are rumbling toward them, shrouding the mountaintop in darkness. Lightning flashes somewhere inside the cloud bank, turning the edges a sickly green for the briefest moment.

"Hurry!" Mara says, sweeping up the tiny girl in her arms and darting forward. "Does anyone see a way up? Anything at all?"

But there is nothing. The walls are nearly sheer now, interrupted by clumps of mesquite. She could climb it. Reynaldo and Adán could too. But the little ones wouldn't stand a chance, and Julio's horse would never make it.

The ground trembles. A jackrabbit bounces across their path, then two more. They fly up the steep bank and disappear into a tiny hole.

"Did you see that?" Adán calls out.

Mara's heart races with the implication. If the animals are fleeing . . .

"Run!" she screams. "Everybody run! Climb up as soon as you can."

The trickle of water they've been following widens to a tiny stream, pushing detritus along with it. They splash through, always looking upward toward the ridge, and Mara dreads seeing one of them go down with a sprained ankle.

"There!" calls out the boy who had been crying only moments before. Mara follows the direction of his pointing finger and doesn't see anything, but a few more steps forward and she does. It's a drainage ditch, cutting through the hill— hardly more than a slight seam in the earth. Water pours down it already, into their ravine, but at a gentle enough slope that with some coaxing and pushing, the little ones might make it up.

"Julio, you go first," she orders. "Quickly!" It's steep and uneven, but a good mountain pony should be able to make it.

Julio clucks to the mare, and she plods forward into the adjoining ravine. His body lists to the right; he's barely holding his seat. Mara almost steps forward to help him, but she can't leave the little ones.

The earth trembles again. "Go! Hurry!" she yells, gesturing the others to follow Julio. Which is when she sees her mistake. By insisting that Julio get to safety first, she has blocked their narrow path. No one can pass the careful mountain pony. No one can hurry.

"You!" she yells to the nearest boy. "Go whack that horse on the rump. Now!" As he scrambles up the drainage ditch after Julio, Mara looks for a place to deposit the tiny girl—a ledge, a bush with a big enough trunk, anything that might be high enough to avoid the quickly rising water. But there is nothing.

Mara's feet are ankle-deep now, and the gusting wind kicks up spray and dust, making it hard to see. Carella's daughter stands at Mara's side, helping her direct the others.

"Now you!" the little girl yells to a much older boy. "Careful of that branch. All right, your turn." One by one the children climb up into the ditch, until only Mara, Carella's daughter, and the tiny girl remain. The water reaches Mara's knees, which means it's to the girl's waist. They won't be able to stand against the current much longer.

"Go now," Mara says to Carella's daughter. "I'll be right behind you." Mara hitches the tiny girl higher on her hip. Somehow, she'll have to make the climb one-handed.

The girl has barely started to climb when a rumbling noise makes her pause. She and Mara look toward the sound. It's a wall of churning, muddy water, tumbling down the mountain toward them.

Mara launches past Carella's daughter up into the ditch. She scrambles over mud and stones, through skin-ripping branches, still looking for a place to tuck the tiny girl.

A head peeks down from around a boulder. It's Reynaldo. "Hand her to me!" he hollers, reaching for her. Mara braces against the side of the ditch so she can lift the tiny girl with both hands. Reynaldo plucks her from Mara's grasp, and Mara darts back down the way she came.

"Mara!" Reynaldo calls.

Below her, Carella's daughter has slipped in the mud to her belly, arms and legs splayed. Her wide eyes are a startling white contrast to her muddy face and hair. "Help!" she cries.

The wall of water is upon them, and Mara has no time to be gentle. She grabs a nearby manzanita branch with one hand; with the other she lunges down, grabs the girl's cold, slick arm, and gives it a tremendous yank.

The girl screams, but the sound is cut off by water filling her mouth and nose.

Mara's arms threaten to rip from her sockets as water sucks the girl down, but she refuses to let go, pulling with all her might. Gradually, the girl's soaked head breaks through the whitewater, then her shoulders. One final tug, and the girl's body is more on the bank than in the water. She lies perfectly still. Blood pours from a gash on the side of her head.

The water level is still rising. Mara stretches farther, hooks the girl's armpit, and drags her up even higher, until only her toes trail in the water. One foot is now bare.

Mara collapses on her back. Her arms are rubbery, and her temples have a sharp, squeezed pain from so much effort. She turns her head to regard the girl beside her, half expecting her to be limp and dead.

The girl convulses once, hard. Then she coughs, and something that is half floodwater, half vomit dribbles from her mouth.

Joy surges in Mara's chest, as brilliant as a rising summer sun. She digs her heels into the mud bank for leverage, then helps the girl sit up. "That's it," she murmurs as the girl continues to heave. "Just cough it all out."

"Is she all right?" It's Reynaldo. He lowers himself to their position, using rocks and scrub for purchase.

"I think so. She has a bad gash on her head. And I may have hurt her when I pulled her out. But . . . I think so." *I saved her.* The truth of this marvelous fact fills her limbs with tingling warmth. Maybe she can save them all.

"We should get moving," Reynaldo warns. "The water is still rising."

The sky chooses that moment to dump vicious streamers of rain, and Mara blinks water from her eyes. "The others? Did they . . ."

"All safe on the ridge."

She breathes relief. "Let's go, then." To Carella's daughter, she says, "Can you climb?"

The girl coughs one more time, but she nods, and Mara marvels at her bravery. She can't be more than five or six, but she stayed behind to help everyone else. Now her lungs must be on fire, her head pounding, her shoulder stinging, but instead of fear or pain in her eyes, Mara sees only determination.

"What's your name?" Mara asks.

"Teena."

"All right, Teena. Let's get up on that ridge, then we'll let you rest."

12

THE tiny girl's name is Marlín. The brothers Reynaldo discovered in the cellar are Benito and Hando. There are also Alessa, Quintoro, Rosa, Marco, and Jaime. They sit huddled on the ridge, shivering in the rain, while Mara checks everyone over. The gash on Teena's head is not deep, so Mara tears a strip from Julio's saddle blanket and uses it to stanch the flow of blood.

"I'm not sure what to do about your shoes," she says to the girl.

Teena shrugs. "I don't need shoes," she says, kicking off her remaining one. Then her face freezes. Her chin trembles.

"What is it?" Mara says. "Are you hurt somewhere else?"

She shakes her head, staring at the discarded shoe. It lies on its side, a leather tassel dragging in the mud. It is worn through at the heel. She has been walking in near-useless shoes the whole time. "Mamá and me, we went to the tanner to get my feet measured. Because I'm so big now. But the bad men came."

"We'll get you some new shoes. It might take a while, but

we'll do it." Even as she says it, Mara knows it won't be enough. It's not the shoes that Teena misses.

"She let herself die on purpose," Teena says, still staring at the shoes. "So we could get away."

Mara's throat tightens. "She loved you very much." She can hardly get the words out. What must it be like to have parents who would sacrifice their own lives for you?

Little Marco has an ugly gash just below his knee. The others seem to be in relatively good shape, though they huddle together in shivering groups, waiting for the rain to stop. Mara grimaces. It's safe enough to have a fire, now that clouds choke the sky. But unless they find shelter, the driving rain makes it impossible.

Quintoro wraps an arm around his little sister, Rosa, who has been quietly crying ever since they escaped the flood. Adán digs at the earth with a stick, poking and shoving in frustrated bursts. Julio sits propped against the trunk of a small cottonwood, eyes closed, his beautiful face raised to the rain. His breathing is shallow, his face pale.

"Everybody up," Mara orders, getting to her feet. "It's too cold to sit still." And too depressing.

"We need rest," Reynaldo says. "The little ones are exhausted."

Mara shakes her head. "We're exposed up here on the ridge. Once the storm is over, we'll be visible to anyone within half a day's travel. So we move now and rest when we find shelter."

Everyone grumbles as they get to their feet. After she helps Julio stand, he wraps his arms around her and leans against her. His skin is feverish, and she can feel the pulse at his neck—fast and fluttery like butterfly wings. "I love you," he says.

"Prove it by getting well," she answers.

She and Adán help him mount the horse. "You should tie me down," Julio says, even as he lists to the right.

Mara swallows hard. Then she mounts up behind him and puts an arm around his waist. He winces at the contact. "I'll hold you," Mara says.

They set off down the mountain. There is no trail, so they must go carefully, slipping through mud and navigating outcroppings and stunted trees. Below them, the fault has become a churning river, thick with mud and detritus. Above, the sky continues to dump rain. Mara wonders if she'll ever be warm and dry again.

She holds Julio close to keep him upright, feeling his heartbeat against her chest. There is no way to avoid the wound on his lower back, and though he is bravely stoic, the occasional jostling step of their mount makes him gasp. She buries her face between his shoulder blades and breathes his scent, wishing she could somehow send her own warmth and vitality into his body.

They walk for hours, until Alessa plunks onto the ground and bursts into tears.

Reynaldo hurries over to her.

"What is it?" Mara calls.

"Her feet," Reynaldo says. "She's been walking with blisters. Now her feet are ripped to shreds."

"My feet hurt too," says Rosa.

"Mine too," says Hando.

Mara takes a deep breath. "Everyone's feet hurt," she says. "But we have to be brave. Alessa, if you promise to hold on to Julio and keep him from falling, you can trade places with me."

Alessa brightens. "I can do that."

The saddle isn't big enough for two adults anyway, and the edge had been digging into Mara's rear. She plants a kiss behind Julio's ear and dismounts, then helps Alessa up behind him.

"Can I ride the horse too?" someone asks.

"Me too!" says another.

Mara is careful to keep her voice calm and patient. "When Alessa's feet are better, everyone can take turns helping Julio."

Hando eyes the other packhorse, but he says nothing. Mara will let the children ride the second horse if she has to, but she's not sure the rest of them are up to carrying the supplies. Not without more food to give them strength.

She takes the lead this time, keeping an eye out for shelter as she goes, but her heart is sinking. She wants to save them. Every single one. She hoped a flash flood would be the worst they encountered. But maybe it will be something little that eventually kills them all. Something insignificant. Like blistered feet.

The clouds are beginning to break and the sun is low on the horizon when Mara spots a large overhang of layered sandstone. The ground beneath is not entirely dry, but it's flat and littered with deadfall that has been trapped there by the wind.

Some of it might be dry enough for a fire.

She sets the children to work collecting wood while she and Adán quickly line a pit. Within an hour, they are crowded around a cheery fire. Several peel off outer clothing layers and drape them on nearby rocks to dry. As the sun edges behind the shattered peak, Mara finds a bit of gladness inside herself, for they are nearly to the bottom of the mountain and will soon move into the desert.

Her flour sack is soaked, and the remaining flour will turn moldy and useless for baking, so she scoops out a bunch of the sticky stuff and stirs it into a potful of boiling water. At least water is no longer in short supply.

She adds bits of bacon and a few of her precious spices. The result is disgusting—more paste than soup, with a gritty texture that sticks in her teeth. But it's nourishing, and even though the children wince and swallow quickly, they don't complain. Everyone goes to sleep without the empty ache of hunger.

They wake to morning sun and screaming.

Mara launches upward, reaching for her bow and seeking the source of danger even before her mind is fully awake. Deep in the overhang, pressed against the sandstone wall, little Hando sobs, clutching his right arm to his stomach.

Rosa stands beside him, looking down in horror. She's the one who is screaming.

"What is it?" Mara demands. "What's wro—"

Something behind Hando moves. No, writhes. Several somethings. Twisting and sliding and . . .

Vipers.

"Be very, very still," she says, though she knows it's too late for him. "Everyone else get back. Now!"

As they hasten to comply, something black and hot clouds Mara's vision. She led them here. She made them take shelter beside a vipers' nest. She should have scouted the site thoroughly before bedding down.

Mara creeps toward Hando, who is as still as a stone though tears leak from his pleading eyes. "That's it, Hando. You're doing fine." Behind him, the vipers mix and tumble like giant worms. She hears the hiss of a rattle.

"I'm going to reach down and snatch you up," she says. "Ready?"

He nods.

Before her pounding heart can become paralyzing terror, she grabs his arms and yanks him backward. His feet drag as she darts from the overhang into a clear blue day.

They need to get farther away. Snakes can move with astonishing speed if they want to. But she only has moments left to save Hando. She compromises, dragging him only a few steps more.

"Show me the bite," she orders. "Everyone else, keep an eye on those snakes! Grab some rocks in case they move toward us."

Hando pushes up his sleeve, revealing a red, swollen spot with two tiny puncture marks just below the elbow. A small snake, then. Maybe he didn't take much venom.

She grabs her knife from her belt, unsheathes it. "This is

going to hurt, but I have to do it now. Understand?"

He nods, lower lip quivering.

Hando hisses as she sweeps her blade across the bite. The skin parts, and blood wells. She gives a quick thought to possible cavities in her teeth but decides it doesn't matter; her larger body can handle the venom much better than his anyway.

She places her lips on his filthy arm, sealing the wound. Closing her eyes against revulsion, she sucks a mouthful of blood. Coppery tanginess bursts warm across her tongue as she turns her head to spit. She sucks again. Spits again.

Hando whimpers as she works. "Kill as many as you can!" someone yells. "But don't get too close." Rocks pound the ground nearby, and she almost looks up to see what's happening, but she forces herself to keep sucking and spitting. The urge to swallow is almost unbearable, even though the taste is revolting.

At last she moves her head away. "Water!" she yells, and a water skin is placed in her hand as if by magic. She rinses and spits several times. Finally she lets herself swallow.

She pours the rest of the water over Hando's arm, then pokes around the wound, encouraging the cleansing blood to flow.

Hando asks in a trembling voice, "Am I going to die?"

Yes, probably. She reaches down to cup his chin and looks him directly in the eye. "If the bite wasn't deep, if the venom was close to the skin, then maybe not. But it will hurt badly for about an hour. It will be the worst hurt you've ever had." Of its own accord, her thumb sweeps along his jawline. "When the pain starts to go away, you'll get sick. I'll need you to be very brave."

He nods up at her. Already his face is sallow and his breath comes fast. He says, "Thank you, Mara."

She gives his chin a gentle squeeze and lets it go. Hando is such a beautiful boy, with a delicate cast to cheek and chin, and eyelashes so thick that his eyes seemed rimmed with kohl. He will break many hearts someday, if he has a chance to grow up.

"We got us some snake meat," Reynaldo says at her shoulder.

She turns to find him holding up a limp viper, its scaled white belly glistening in the sunshine, and she flinches back.

"How many did you kill?"

He grins. "Five."

Heat spreads across her neck and shoulders, and she can't seem to get enough air. Some venom got inside her after all. Or maybe her body is merely rebelling against the fact that these children risked their lives so they could eat well tonight.

13

MARA unloads the second packhorse and distributes every-thing among the remaining healthy children to carry. Then she helps Hando mount, hoping and praying that no one else becomes injured, for they are out of horses.

By nightfall, his arm has swollen to twice its size. Everyone else feasts on roasted snake, but Hando can't keep anything down. He thrashes on the ground, moaning, only half conscious.

She checks Alessa's feet. They are badly blistered, but the blisters seem to have drained well, and Alessa claims they only hurt when she walks. Mara orders her to keep them clean.

Next she settles beside Julio. He lies on his side by the fire, unable to sit up. "Hello, beautiful," he whispers weakly.

She traces his lips with her forefinger. "I have to check your back."

He nods.

Carefully, she unwraps the bandages. The entry site has puffed out like a cauliflower, and something that is part blood, part pus leaks from the gash. It's badly infected, in spite of her earlier efforts. If they don't get help soon, he'll die.

"How bad is it?" he says between gritted teeth.

Mara is glad the dark hides her tears. "I think it's getting better."

"Liar."

She rewraps the wound. There is nothing she can do for it.

He says, "If I don't make it, promise me—"

"You'll make it!" Her voice comes out angrier than she intends.

"Mara. Love. This is a bad wound. A death wound. I need to know you'll look out for Adán."

"I . . . of course." Then she reaches over to flick his nose. "But I'm not giving up yet, you idiot."

He grins. Then his eyes flutter closed, and she hopes with all the hope in her heart that it's a natural sleep and not a sickly one.

14

IT rains again the next day, but Mara orders them up and moving anyway.

"A day's rest wouldn't hurt," Adán says, as she fills her water skin with brown runoff water.

"We're exhausted," Reynaldo agrees. "And the little ones had a big fright with those snakes."

Mara shakes her head. "We have to find help soon," she says. "If we don't travel, Julio and Hando will die. Maybe all of us."

Adán and Reynaldo exchange a look, but they say nothing more.

Within an hour, they are covered in mud and chilled to the bone. Rosa complains again that her feet hurt. Quintoro is hungry. Tiny Marlín, toddling barefoot beside her, begins to cry softly.

Mara looks down and frowns. "Marlín? What's the matter?" Of all of them, she is the one who has complained the least. But somewhere along the way, she lost her shoes. Or maybe she never had any. Not every child in the village had good shoes.

The little girl sniffs. "Muffin was *not* bad."

"Muffin . . . Oh. Your goat?"

Marlín nods. "Mamá said she was a bad goat. Because she ate our carrots. But she wasn't bad. Just hungry. Like me. She had to be outside in the mud a lot. Do you think her feet hurt all the time? If I have another goat, I will make shoes for her."

Mara sighs. "Would you like me to carry you for a while?"

Marlín reaches chubby arms up, and Mara hoists her onto her hip. They've gone several steps when Marlín says quietly, "She screamed."

"Who?"

"Muffin. When the fire came."

"Oh." Mara snugs her a bit closer. "I know you miss Muffin, but I need you to be brave for just a little while longer, all right?"

"All right."

Such an ordinarily simple task lies before them—get from one place to another. But they are in bad shape. She catalogs their injuries: Julio's arrow wound, Hando's bite, the gash on Teena's head, Alessa's badly blistered feet, and now this tiny girl who has been walking barefoot through mud and mesquite for who knows how long. How will she keep them all going?

Mercifully, the slope levels off a bit as they near the desert floor, and Mara lets her eyes rove the jagged desolation below them. It's a warren of buttes and gullies that glow coppery red in the sun, almost as far as the eye can see. Beyond it lies the deeper desert, a sea of sand, but at this distance it is only a yellowish haze on the horizon.

The place is as barren as it is beautiful, yet the nomads of Joya d'Arena make their home here. And she will, too, if they're to have any chance of surviving this war.

"I should lead from here," Reynaldo says.

"It's a maze down there," Mara says. "No wonder the rebels chose this for their hideout."

"Someone should hang back and make sure we're not followed," he adds. "The perimeter watch won't let us pass if there is any chance we've led the Inviernos to their camp."

The back of her neck prickles. She had not considered that their enemy might follow them unseen. "Any volunteers?" she asks.

"I'll do it," says Adán.

"No!" She needs him nearby and safe, for Julio's sake. "I . . . er . . . I may need help carrying the little ones, and you're the strongest."

"I can do it," says another boy. He is the next oldest after Adán, a quiet one who prefers whittling with his knife to conversation.

She searches her memory for his name and snags it. "Thank you, Benito. Don't hang back too far—it will be easy to get lost once we're down there."

His lips turn up in a cocky half smile. "I'll be fine," he says, and then he disappears into the brush.

Reynaldo leads them west, away from the Shattermount's flooded fault line. The sky is still drizzly and gray, their journey slippery with mud. Marlín grows heavy in her arms.

Late in the afternoon, the sun breaks through the clouds,

sending streamers of gold onto the earth and causing a bright rainbow that stretches the length of two days' journey. They exchange relieved smiles and pick up the pace. They will rue the relentless desert sun soon enough, but for now they glory in the way it steams away the soaked terrain.

Reynaldo calls a halt. At Mara's questioning look, he says, "Did you hear something?"

Mara orders everyone to silence. Quietly, she lowers Marlín to the ground, then stretches her aching arms as she listens for anything unusual.

"Mara!" comes the voice, faintly. "Help!"

"Is that Benito?" Adán asks, but Mara is already sprinting back the way they came, swinging her bow from her shoulder.

She hears the sounds of struggle before she finds them— crunching gravel, a grunt, a sharp yell of pain. She nearly trips on them as they roll around in a tangle of hair and limbs. Yellow hair snarled with black, pale skin against dark. The Invierno's anklet bones rattle as they wrestle in the mud.

There's no way she'll get a clean shot. Her hand flies to the knife at her belt, but their grappling bodies move so fast, and she doesn't trust herself not to stab Benito by mistake.

The Invierno's yellow braid whips around, and she sees her chance. She lunges into the fray, grabs the end of the braid, yanks it hard. He yelps, his head snapping back. Benito takes advantage and sends a fist into his stomach, then another. He rolls the Invierno onto his back and starts to pound at his face. Something crunches.

"Benito, that's enough." Mara's belly squirms with wrongness.

But the boy is blind with fear and rage, and he sends his fist crashing into the enemy's jaw, his ear, his eye.

"Benito!" she yells.

A shape blurs past her. It's Adán. With a roar, he plunges his skinning knife into the Invierno's chest. Mara senses the other children coming up behind her, even as Adán wrenches his blade from the Invierno's bloody chest and raises it to strike again.

"No!" Mara darts forward, grabs Adán's arm. "Stop!"

Adán lashes out blindly with his other hand. His knuckles crack against her cheek, and she tumbles backward, landing hard on her rear.

Red spots dance in her vision as her eye socket blossoms with pain.

"Oh, God. Mara, I'm so sorry. I . . . oh, God." Adán throws his knife away from himself and stares at his hands as though they belong to a stranger. Spatters of blood cover his shirt.

Mara gets shakily to her feet. "Adán and Benito," she says, her voice like thunder. "You are responsible for this, therefore you will dispose of this body."

"He surprised me!" Benito says. "We stumbled onto each other, and all of a sudden, he was on top of me, and I—"

She holds up a silencing hand. "If more scouts discover him, they will know we passed this way. So you will bury him thoroughly and clean up any blood. The rest of us will set up camp and wait for you."

Soft crying trickles up to her ears, and Mara looks down to see Marlín at her elbow, the girl's horrified gaze fixed on the bloody corpse of the Invierno. Mara bends over and picks her up. "I need you to be brave for me, Marlín," she says.

Marlín sniffs. "You say that a lot."

"Only because it's the truest thing I know right now."

"No fire tonight," Reynaldo says. "There could be more scouts nearby."

"Did he track us, do you think?" Mara asks. They haven't even bothered to disguise their trail.

"I doubt it," Reynaldo says. "But after we break camp tomorrow, we should get rid of any footprints, cover the site with brush. Try to make it look like we were never here."

"Good thinking." To Benito and Adán, she says, "No shallow grave. We don't want coyotes digging him up."

"You're punishing us," Benito says. "Even though he is the enemy!"

Mara stares him down. "You and Adán were not wrong to kill. This is war, after all. But you were wrong to lose control. Join us in camp only when you're certain you have it back again."

Mara has survived this long only by remaining in control. If she is going to keep these children alive, they will have to learn it too.

15

THEY haven't eaten in two days. They have all thinned noticeably, no one more so than Julio. His cheeks are gaunt, and his
eyes are dark, sunken shadows in his otherwise pallid face. At
least once per hour, someone complains about hunger.

Mara begins to practice with her bow in the evenings and
early mornings. Several of the others have slings, and she makes
them train together. She tells them they all need to practice so
they can hunt as they go. But really, she needs something to
distract them from their aching, empty bellies.

And she knows that if they encounter another Invierno
scout, she'll need more skill with the bow to protect them. She
practices a quick draw and notch, over and over. Next, she'll
teach herself to hit a moving target.

"Where did you get that bow?" Reynaldo asks her one
morning. They have stepped away from the campsite while
the others linger over hot tea. Mara used some of the precious
herbs from her satchel to make it. Anything to fool their stomachs for a little while.

"Pá got it for me as a Deliverance Day gift," she says, as she sights a withered pinecone that she placed atop a boulder.

"It must have been expensive," he says wonderingly. "It's beautiful wood. Someone would have had to go high into the Sierra Sangre for that quality of pine."

She lets her arrow fly. It misses the target by a handspan at least, and she frowns. "Arrows don't come cheap either. I think that's why he got it. He didn't actually like the idea of me *using* it. He just wanted to show off his wealth at a time when all the village children were practicing with their slings."

Reynaldo studies her thoughtfully. "I shouldn't speak ill of the dead, but . . ."

Mara raises an eyebrow at him. "A dead priest, no less."

His gaze is slightly shifted, as if he can't quite bring himself to look her in the eye. It's the scar on the corner of her eyelid he's avoiding, the one her father gave her when she was ten years old. "But he was not a good man, was he?" he says.

"No, he was not."

Reynaldo winds up with his sling and throws. His loosed pebble arcs toward the pinecone, but drops too soon and thunks against the boulder instead. "One time my má was sick," he says, seeming not to notice how badly he just missed. "Bad sick. And your pá rode hard all night to get to our farmstead in time to sit the death watch. He tended her himself. Forced her to sip her tea, changed out wet cloths for her forehead. And come morning, her fever broke and she was fine."

Mara clenches her jaw, not sure how to respond. Yes, her father was known for acts of tremendous kindness. She came to see them as pretense. Little deceptions meant to cover up the truth of their lives.

But hearing Reynaldo talk about it, she can't help but wonder if they were genuine after all. In the same way that the best lies have an element of truth, maybe evil is made all the more powerful when it is accompanied by the startling presence of grace. She says, "He was a good man too. In some ways. That's what made him so terrifying."

Reynaldo stares openly now, as if seeing her scar for the first time. Mara always thought it made her look perpetually sad, or at least tired. Until Julio assured her it gave her a sultry air, like she had just been thoroughly kissed. What does Reynaldo see?

"Mara!" someone calls out. "Come quick!" The voice is edged with panic.

She sprints back toward the campsite without a moment's hesitation, Reynaldo at her heels.

The children are gathered around something. Mara leaps over the fire pit and elbows them out of the way, demanding, "What is it? What's wro . . ."

It's Julio. He has fallen over, and his cheek grinds into the earth as he gasps for breath. Beside him, a wooden bowl lies overturned in a tiny, muddy puddle of sage tea.

Mara drops to the ground beside him. "Julio?" She places her fingertips at his neck and is relieved to find a weak, scattered pulse.

"He started shaking," Alessa says, tears in her voice. "Then he dropped his bowl and fell over, but he wouldn't stop twitching, and then—" Someone shushes her.

Julio's eyelids flutter open. "Mara," he whispers. "My Mara."

"Is it the pain? I'll make you some more tea. We need to make sure you're getting enough to drink. Then I'll—"

His hand traps hers, brings it against his chest with surprising strength. His skin is as hot and dry as the desert sun. "No. Just . . . sit with me, please."

She blinks rapidly. "Don't you dare give up. Don't you *dare*."

He sighs. "Promise me you'll—"

"Yes. Adán. I know. But you have to promise not to give up."

Julio tries to speak but can't. He takes a few breaths. Tries again. "Not him. *You*. Promise me you won't hate the world."

She shakes her head. "I . . . Oh, Julio."

He smiles. "You burn so bright, Mara."

He's too weak to say anything else. They sit there for a moment, staring into each other's eyes. She doesn't see the Julio in front of her—only the Julio from the meadow, carefree and confident, full of exuberant words and all kinds of plans. Her only plan, her only hope, was *him*.

Then his hand drops away, plops onto the ground where it lies limply. His head rolls to the side. The light fades from his eyes.

"Julio?" She grabs his limp hand and squeezes. "No, no, no, no." She kisses his knuckles, over and over again. Her tears make muddy streaks on his skin. "Julio, you have to fight. Don't give up. Please, I need—"

A hand settles on her shoulder. "He's gone, Mara," Reynaldo says.

But Julio's hand is still warm. How can he be dead when his hand is still warm? It's like her insides are splitting open. *No, no, no, no.*

"Mara?" The voice comes from far away. Another world. Another life.

She stretches out beside Julio, rubs her hands up and down his arm, gazes upon his beautiful but colorless face.

"Mara!"

"Go," she says, not taking her eyes off of Julio. "Just go."

"He wouldn't want you to be like this." Adán's voice this time.

"I don't care."

"Didn't you promise to take care of me?" His voice turns plaintive and high, like he's a small boy instead of nearly a man. "You promised. I know you did."

She looks up. His face is wet with tears, and he is half bent over with a pain of his own.

Mara did promise. And she meant it, so she ought to make good. But she feels as though a chunk of her own self has been cruelly excised, leaving only pain. "I don't know how . . ." she sobs out. "I can't . . ." Maybe part of her died with Julio, and the rest longs to follow.

Arms wraps around her. Then more, and still more, until she is at the hot, heavy center of a dozen pairs of embracing limbs.

"*We'll* carry *you* for a bit," Reynaldo says. "It's our turn."

And they do. Reynaldo and Adán heave Julio's body across the packhorse and tie him down. Then they brace Mara—one under each arm—and lift her from the ground.

Tiny Marlín plants herself in their path. She reaches up and pats Mara's hip. *Pat, pat. Patpatpat.* Her face is a mask of solemnity.

She says, "I need you to be a brave girl for me, Mara."

Mara doesn't know how to respond. Marlín steps aside, and Reynaldo and Adán hold Mara up. She hangs limp between them.

They're about to step forward, but Mara says, "Wait."

They wait.

Mara gathers her feet beneath her. She leans over and gives Reynaldo a kiss on the cheek, then does the same to Adán. "Thank you," she says, straightening. "But I can walk on my own."

16

THE next day, Reynaldo says they have gone as far as he can take them. Now all they can do is wander around until the perimeter guard finds them.

There is no indication that anyone is near, no sign of life or habitation, but one moment they're skirting a huge butte of layered sandstone, and the next, two young men materialize as if by magic in their path.

"Who are you?" one demands, his hand on the hilt of a hunting knife at his belt.

Reynaldo whispers, "We've made it."

"Refugees," Mara tells them. "Our village was destroyed by Inviernos."

The boys eye them warily. Their collective gaze roves over Julio's body, draped over the packhorse, but their expression gives away nothing.

Reynaldo steps forward. "I am cousin to Humberto and Cosmé. I have a standing invitation to join your cause, and these are my companions."

"Were you followed?"

Reynaldo doesn't even blink. "We were. But we took care of it."

The boys exchange a glance. One nods at the other and says, "I'll take a look. Tell the others we need to extend the perimeter for a few days."

As he melts back into the scrub, the remaining boy says, "This way. Keep quiet."

They are led through a maze of twisting ravines and choking bramble. Mara considers that the boy might be leading them in a roundabout way on purpose. If so, it's a smart plan, because she is well and truly lost in moments. Marlín's tiny hand slips into hers, and she gives it a reassuring squeeze. "Do you need me to carry you?" she whispers down to the girl.

"No. I'm a big girl now," she says.

The ravine opens into a small vale. Figures appear on the ridge above, surrounding them, just like the Inviernos who attacked their village. Mara has a moment's panic.

But instead of attacking, they pour down the slope. Some smile in greeting. Only a few have weapons—all sheathed. They are children, mostly. Clean, well-fed, healthy.

These perfect strangers take their hands, murmur words of welcome. One young man lodges himself under Hando's good shoulder and supports him the rest of the way.

A beautiful girl with short, curly hair takes charge. She lifts the corner of the blanket covering Julio's body and says, "Too late for this one. Take him to the other side of the butte." Someone grabs the reins to the packhorse and leads it away.

Mara swallows hard, but does not protest.

"This one needs an amputation immediately," the beautiful girl says when she sees Hando's black-streaked forearm. "Head gash here will need stitches," she says of Teena. "Too late to treat your burn," she tells Marco. "But maybe some salve will help." Mara hadn't realized Marco had been burned; he never complained.

One by one she goes through each member of their party, directing others to action, until finally she reaches Mara. "You've been though a lot," she says, her head cocked quizzically.

Mara shrugs. "It's war."

The girl nods. "I'm Cosmé. Welcome to our camp. If you betray us, I'll kill you."

"If you betray me or these children, I'll kill you first."

Cosmé flashes a grin. She indicates a general direction with her head. "Head over to the cavern if you want some hot stew." And then she's off, tending to the wounded.

An old man with a missing arm approaches next. "You are Mara, the leader of this group, yes?"

"I guess."

He reaches up and clutches her shoulder. "I am Father Alentín, priest to these wayward miscreants, and you, dear girl, are most welcome. Come, I'll show you the way."

As they head up the slope together, Mara says, "Everyone here seems so . . . healthy."

"Compared to recent refugees, I suppose," he says with a sad smile. "We're managing. Lots of wounded, though. We lose someone almost every day. But!" His grin becomes enormous.

"This war may have just taken a turn for the better."

They crest the rise, and Mara looks out on a small but beautiful village of adobe *hutas* built into the side of an enormous butte. Just beyond, the butte curves inward, resulting in a massive half cavern that is open to the sky but sheltered from the worst of wind and rain.

"What do you mean by a turn for the better?" she asks. Looking at this bright, warm place, she can almost believe it.

"We found the bearer, you see," he says. "God's chosen one. There."

Mara follows the direction of his pointing finger and sees two people standing on the highest point of the ridge—a boy with wild hair, and a plump girl with a thick braid. The boy doesn't look like anything special. Intelligent and sturdy, maybe, with a roundness to his features that gives him an air of perpetual surprise.

As Mara and the priest approach, he leans over and whispers, "Her name is Elisa. She is a princess of Orovalle, and we stole her right out from under the nose of His Majesty King Alejandro, may sweet wisdom drop from his lips as honey from the comb."

The chosen one is a *girl*? Mara peers closer.

She can't be more than sixteen years old, and she seems out of place in this harsh desert. Her limbs are too soft, her gaze too wide with horror and shock. But her pretty brown eyes spark, and there's a stubborn set to her lips that makes Mara wonder.

The princess stares as they come face-to-face. Stares hard

and with keen interest, the way Julio always did. And just like with Julio, she is compelled to fill the silence. "I'm Mara," she says. She's not sure what makes her add, "Thank you for coming."

Mara feels the girl's eyes on her back as she heads into the half cavern. Somehow, in this moment, Mara knows that nothing about her will go unnoticed ever again.

17

SHE has barely gone from sunshine to shadow when Teena thrusts a bowl of stew at her. Mara is stunned for a moment as she breathes in the scent of venison. It's so thick, with huge chunks of meat. Even carrots. And suddenly Mara's lips are on the side of the bowl and warm, generous stuff is sliding down her throat, filling her stomach. It leaks past her mouth, smears her cheeks and chin, but she doesn't care.

"That's what I did!" Teena says, laughing. "But then my belly hurt."

Mara forces herself to stop and take a breath. Stew drips from her chin to the ground. She looks around to find the other children slurping with equal abandon, especially tiny Marlín, who sits cuddling her bowl, her eyes closed in perfect ecstasy. For the first time in days, Mara smiles.

"They've already assigned huts to us so we can rest," Teena says brightly. "You get to share with me. They even gave us some blankets. Do you want me to take you there?"

A hut. Rest. Blankets. Words that feel like home.

Mara takes another, less hurried sip of stew. Across the cavern, the beautiful girl Cosmé is tending to Hando's arm, preparing it for amputation. Belén, the boy she briefly loved before she met Julio, interviews the children, trying to find matches with friends or relatives who might already be in their camp. Mara was relieved when he left the village last year, but she's surprised at how glad she is to see him now.

Even the princess is busy, carrying buckets of water from the pool to the infirmary area.

These rebels are people of accord. Of purpose.

Mara throws back her shoulders, as if by doing so she can shake off their long journey, her father's abuse, Julio's death. It's not enough. The memories will cling stubbornly, maybe forever, but she finds that she can stand under their weight after all.

Teena peers at her questioningly, for she has been silent too long.

She takes a deep, cleansing breath. Her hope can't come from Julio anymore. She must nurture it inside herself, and she must fill it with purpose. Mara says, "Thank you, Teena, but not just yet. Do you know where the kitchen area is? I want to get to work right away."

THE KING'S
GUARD

1

THE morning sun crawls over the palace wall when I enter the training yard for recruit selection. I'm the first one here, not because there is honor in being first, but because I have the shortest distance to come. I already live in the palace.

I carry three items; Royal Guard recruits are allowed exactly three possessions from their previous lives. We give up everything else—title, property, and loyalty to anyone other than our king—for the privilege of joining the most elite fighting force in all of Joya d'Arena. Or I guess I should say the *chance* of joining; being a recruit is no guarantee of making the cut.

I don't wait long before the other recruits begin to arrive, their own three items in hand. They are all older than I am, taller, stronger. Most have served a year or two in countship guards, a few in the army. All of them keep their distance. They expect me to fail, partly because I'm only fifteen years old, but mostly because I didn't make it to recruit training on my own merit. I'm here as a special favor to the king.

For two years I ran errands in the palace. I stood at King Nicolao's side when he met with condes and ambassadors, dictated reports, and discussed strategy with his aides. When I wasn't with the king, I served Prince Alejandro, and eventually I became his squire. Now Alejandro is king, and I have asked him for a boon.

"All I want," I told him, "is the opportunity to prove myself."

Even he believes that I am too young for the Guard, too inexperienced, and he suggested I wait a few years. But I'm tired of waiting.

The iron portcullis slams down, locking us in.

Lord-Commander Enrico strides toward us, dressed in shining armor, the red cloak that marks him as Royal Guard whipping at his heels. He is one of the tallest and most polished men I've ever known. His clothes are always impeccable, and the curls of his hair are oiled to shine. He's a commoner by birth, though rumor throughout the palace is that he has aspirations of true nobility and fancies himself a player in the game of politics.

"Form a line!" yells Commander Enrico.

We run to comply. The training yard is a massive oval with dusty, hard-packed ground surrounded on all sides by a stone wall. At one end are straw practice dummies and archery targets. At the other, a dark archway leads to the barracks. Several Royal Guardsmen lean against the portcullis, arms crossed, faces amused. Sitting on the wall on either side is a gathering crowd: Royal Guard, palace guard, city watch, and even a handful of young noblewomen. Everyone has come to gawk at the new recruits.

Usually, the king comes to watch recruiting day too. I asked him not to, just this once. There's no way I could stand here at attention being gawked at without catching Alejandro's amused gaze. No way I could pretend he wasn't sitting out in the open, dangerously exposed. And I really, really need to pretend he's not a factor today. That he is not, in fact, my good friend.

Enrico walks the length of our line, arms behind his back, eyebrow raised in either contempt or challenge. The first recruits he addresses are Tomás and Marlo of the city watch, recommended by General Luz-Manuel himself. They are about twenty years old, with nice full mustaches and the ease of stance that comes with being the best at everything they've ever done. Enrico welcomes them warmly.

If they're going to be the commander's favorites, it would be smart for me to get to know them.

Enrico pauses next before a lean young man with dark skin and quick eyes. He wears ragged homespun, and his right shoe has a hole in the toe. He carries a bow, a quiver, and a bundle of arrows as his chosen items, not realizing that the Guard will give him better weapons.

"Fernando de Ismelda," Enrico says. "You won the kingdom's archery competition. I gather it was quite a surprise to everyone."

"Not to me," the boy says.

I decide that I like Fernando de Ismelda.

But Enrico frowns. He is silent a long time, trying to make Fernando uncomfortable. Finally, he says, "It's true that the Royal Guard is a place where men of station as low as yours can rise to the highest ranks in the kingdom, based on their own merits. But you'll find that much more is required than just being a good shot."

Lord-Commander Enrico moves on to the young man standing beside me, a giant with hands like paddles. "And you are?" he says.

"Lucio, my lord," the young man answers.

Enrico nods. "Ah, yes, former squire to Conde Treviño. I've heard good things about you, son."

"Thank you, my lord."

Either Enrico is getting bad information, or he's being deliberately false to test the rest of us. We've all heard of Lucio of Basajuan, a notorious bully with a penchant for drunken watch shifts. One of his three items is an amphora of wine, which he slings one-handed the way most men would carry a jug. Surely, someone advised him against that. Just as surely, Lucio ignored them.

I'm not the only one who is here as a favor to a powerful man. Lucio is the youngest son of Conde Treviño's wealthiest supporter, and the conde found it problematic to discipline him without offending the boy's father. So Lucio was sent to the Royal Guard either as a last-ditch attempt at reform or as a way of washing him out of the conde's service without blame.

Enrico sizes me up last. Sweat trickles down my temples,

and my three possessions grow heavy in my arms. I'm not sure what he's waiting for. Maybe he's testing me under the burden of silence. I've seen how waiting, how not knowing, can break a man. But not me. Enrico can stare as much as he wants.

"You are Hector de Ventierra, yes?" Enrico says coldly. "Third son of Conde Ricardón de Ventierra?"

I stare straight ahead, focusing on the king's crest, which flaps in the breeze above the portcullis. But the sun catches on the commander's bronze epaulets, flashing fire in my eyes, and I can't help but wince.

"Just Hector now, my lord," I say.

He knows perfectly well who I am. He is Alejandro's personal guard and I'm his squire. We've rubbed shoulders countless times.

"Just *recruit* now. The Guard is a place for *men* who work and get things done, not for lordlings eager to play at being soldier. What did you bring with you, boy?"

"A blanket, my lord."

"Why did you bring a blanket?"

"The recruit quarters are said to be cold, my lord."

"That thing looks more like a dress for a princess ball."

Several of the recruits snicker. This is a trick. He didn't ask a question, so I am not supposed to answer.

Alejandro warned me that the recruit barracks is really a dungeon that gets too chilly for our one-blanket allotment. So Queen Rosaura, who is bedridden with a difficult pregnancy, made me a quilt. It's bright and shimmering, a patchwork of scraps from old gowns, and it would indeed look perfect on the bed of a princess. It's guaranteed to earn me a thrashing or two, but Rosaura is one of the best people in the world, and bringing it seemed like the right thing to do.

"What's that on top of your dress, princess?" Enrico says.

"A memento from my brother's ship, my lord."

My brother's wife, Aracely, gave it to me. It's a decorative plaque made of sea-smoothed ship planking. Burn-etched into the wood are the words, "Harsh winds, rough seas, still hearts." Tiny pinkish shells are arranged into a border around the edges. Hidden within each shell is a jeweled bead. It's a small fortune, a hedge against an uncertain future. "No man or woman should be wholly dependent on another," she said. "If the Guard doesn't work out, or if you ever decide you need to escape, this will give you something to start over with."

"So," Enrico says. "Our princess is homesick for his big brother."

Again, a statement, not a question. I do not reply, though several retorts suggest themselves. *If the hardest thing I have to do is listen to you talk, then I can do that all day, my lord.*

He points to the third item. "A book! You brought a book?"

"Yes, my lord." It's not a manuscript, but an actual bound book about the architectural history of Joya d'Arena. A gift from my mother. The last several pages are blank. I can write whatever I want in them.

"You expect to be so bored here, to have so much free time, that you will be able to read books at your leisure, like priests in a monastery. Do I look like I run a monastery?"

"Not last feast day, when you brought in a wagonload of harlots."

In my defense, he did ask me a question.

I expect a blow. A scolding at least. The crowd is silent, expectant. Drying sweat itches on my cheek, but I refuse to scratch, reminding myself that I can handle it. I can handle anything.

"Make no mistake," Enrico says finally. "I never would have accepted your application were it not for the king's order. I expect you will be expelled within a month."

His forthrightness makes me bold. "I expect you will be surprised, my lord."

"It'll happen within a day if you don't learn to hold your tongue and know your place." He turns and speaks loudly to the whole line. "The king always shows up to view the Guard recruits on the first day. But he didn't today. And do you know why? It's because he didn't want to see his pretty little princess fail."

My face burns. But in a way I feel relieved. Enrico has said the thing everyone is thinking, and it's like a hot, tight blanket has been lifted from the training yard and everyone can breathe. Or maybe just me.

Lord-Commander Enrico steps back, draws his sword, and raises it to the sky. Loudly enough for the whole city to hear, he yells, "Do you have what it takes to be Royal Guard?"

"Yes, my lord!" we answer in unison.

The Guards lounging by the portcullis snigger to one another.

"Can you work harder than you've ever worked—through pain, through pride, through exhaustion—to become something more?"

"Yes, my lord!"

"Will you give up everything you own, everything you are, and swear to protect the king and his interests even unto death?"

"YES, MY LORD!"

His eyes narrow to slits, and he says in a normal voice, "We shall see." He sheathes the sword, sending it home with a *swick!* of finality.

He indicates the portcullis with a lift of his chin, and one of the guards lounging there peels off and steps toward us. "This is Captain Mandrano, my second-in-command," Enrico says of the approaching guard. "He'll play nurse to you whelps for the rest of the day. You will follow his orders without question, as if they come from the king himself. Or"—he stares directly at me—"you will be sent home."

The worst is over. Now I'll be able to show them what I'm worth.

2

THE iron portcullis squeals as it rises, and once Enrico has passed into the cool shadows of the barracks, it slams down behind him with a clang.

Odd. I've watched recruiting day for the Royal Guard for years, even before it became my plan to join. The lord-commander himself always oversees the first day's evaluations. Always.

Captain Mandrano paces before us with hard purpose. He is a beast, with boulders for shoulders and tree trunks for arms. A white scar bisects the right half of his mouth, lifting his lip into a permanent sneer, but a steady intelligence in his eyes gives me hope. This is a man I can impress, a man who will *see*.

The first thing the captain will do is put us through a series of exercises to assess our speed and strength, our coordination and reaction time, our judgment. It happens every year. Sometimes, one or two recruits are cut on the very first day. It's the reason people line the wall, turning the training yard into an arena.

The archer—Fernando—shifts uncomfortably, but I breathe deep through my nose to steady my pulse and send life into my limbs. *Harsh winds, rough seas, still hearts.*

Captain Mandrano's voice booms over our heads. "Your first task," he says, "will be to wash the training yard."

I almost drop my princess quilt.

"What?" Lucio says. Then he goes stiff beside me, and no one wishes he could suck the word back in more than I do.

"Are you questioning orders, whelp?" Mandrano barks.

"No, my lord!"

"Am I wearing gold and jewels? Do I smell like a courtesan's underskirt?"

Lucio hesitates. "No, my lord."

"Then why would you mistake *me* for a *lord*? I'm a workingman who earns my bread, just like every other man in the Royal Guard. Are you a lord?"

He's speaking to Lucio, but I know—everyone here knows—the question is directed at me. I hold my breath and pray that Lucio doesn't make things worse.

"N-No, my . . . captain," Lucio stammers. I allow myself to exhale.

"I'm glad to hear that," Mandrano says. He turns his head and glowers at the whole line of recruits. "All of you workingmen will now wash the walls, as well as the yard."

This time, no one so much as twitches.

"You'll be provided with buckets, soap, and rags. When the monastery bells ring the dinner hour, I'll come to inspect your work. If it has been done to my satisfaction, you'll take your meal in the barracks. Now, get to work!"

Buckets sloshing with lye-murky water are lowered down the wall. A pile of rags tumbles down after them. Everything comes from the direction of the palace laundry, which means they made all the arrangements ahead of time.

I set my quilt, my plaque, and my book on the ground, and head toward the buckets. A moment later, I sense the other boys at my back. As I'm reaching down for the rope handle of the nearest bucket, I hear a voice at my shoulder.

"Wash the training yard?" Fernando whispers. "This whole place will be a muddy mess. It makes no sense."

"Have you ever served in the military, even a local guard?" I ask.

"No. My father's a tanner." He bends down to grab his own bucket. "When I won the king's purse with my bow, Papá told me to try for the Guard—he said I'd be set for life and never have to work as hard as he does."

"Well, that order was not supposed to make sense. We're to follow it anyway." I heave the bucket upward. Water sloshes onto the toes of my boots. Between the fraying rope of the handle and the lye in the water, it will be a wonder if all the skin doesn't peel from my hands. "The sooner we demonstrate that we've learned the lesson, the sooner—"

A heavy blow to my right shoulder spins me around, and I almost drop the bucket. "You're the reason for this," says Lucio, his face dark.

I peer up at him, able to observe him closely for the first time. His eyes are angry. No, rageful. And his rage has a weight about it, as if he's been shoring it up, cultivating it, for a long, long time. And now he's found a focus for it. Lucky me.

"Maybe I am," I admit. Lucio's face flickers with hesitation. I guess that wasn't the response he was expecting. "Or maybe," I continue unwisely, because I can't help it, "all this is meant to wean you from Conde Treviño's teat."

I see the first blow coming and dodge—directly into his second swing. Light bursts across my vision as my neck snaps to the side. I blink. Blink again. Somehow, I ended up flat on my back, twitching in the now-soaked dirt.

Lucio raises his knee. I roll away from his kick. Grab the now-empty bucket. He kicks again, but I raise the bucket just in time. Lucio's foot rips it out of my hands, but he screams in pain. I hope he broke a toe or two.

I scramble to my feet. Blood pours from my head and down my cheek, but so long as it misses my eyes, I'll be fine. I drop into a fighting crouch and size up my options. The other recruits have stepped back to give us space. People along the wall are whooping and hollering like it's a Deliverance Day spectacle.

Lucio's head is lowered, like a bull ready to charge.

I have no weapons. Maybe I could leap onto the wall and grab a dagger from an onlooker. But I don't really think my life is in danger, and I don't want to hurt him badly. A blow to the head with the edge of a bucket is my best option.

But Lucio doesn't charge. Instead, he seems to be thinking.

Damn. I had hoped he wasn't much of a thinker. Then again, a thinking man can be reasoned with.

"Maybe we should get to work," I say carefully. "Start with the walls. We'd get rid of all these spectators if we tossed soapy water onto the walls."

"You insulted me," Lucio says.

"Get used to it. We'll have to bravely face down a lot of dangerous insults before we're allowed to take our oaths."

His fists clench, and I curse myself for stupidity. *Control yourself, Hector.*

I glance around for our captain. Mandrano is by the portcullis, his arms crossed, evaluating us. *Have we failed already, Captain? Are you itching to tell your lord-commander about this?*

If I win here against Lucio, I might fail in reaching my goal, so I drop my guard. "You can thrash me after dinner if you want. But let's get this done first. Either we wash the training yard, or they wash us out."

A muscle in Lucio's jaw twitches. "You're afraid of me."

"Yes," I say, wiping a bit of blood from my temple. "But I'm more afraid of getting cut."

Fernando steps between us, a bucket in hand. "All right, then," he says. "Let's get to work." And he tosses the water against the wall, purposely splashing the dangling legs of several of the palace garrison, who quickly scuttle back and drop out of sight.

We scrub every speck of those walls while the sun beats down on our heads. Then more buckets appear, and we start our useless work on the ground itself. The skin of my hands burns, and the cut on my head stings with sweat.

Much later, the low, orange sun casts gloom onto the training yard, making it hard to tell which areas are damp with water and which are dark with shadows. The monastery bells toll the dinner hour, and I look up from scrubbing uselessly at dirt to find Captain Mandrano standing over me, fists on his hips.

I blink sweat from my eyes and await his pronouncement. Even through my pants, the skin of my knees is rubbed raw, and my lower back aches. My stomach rumbles loudly.

Mandrano smiles, and his scar makes it a mocking grin. "The lot of you had all day to clean the training yard," he says, and his voice and gaze seem to focus on me, "and not one of you thought to wash the dummies or the targets. Is that what you think of the Royal Guard? That it does half a job, then quits?"

The soldiers, Tomás and Marlo, shout, "No, my captain!" and carry their buckets toward the south end of the yard.

Mandrano moves away, continuing his inspection. I rise from my knees, sensing Lucio and Fernando at my shoulders. I hope I don't get saddled with them, as neither is likely to make the cut.

"I could use a glass of wine," Lucio says under his breath.

"I'd be happy with water and a crust of bread," Fernando replies.

Mandrano makes a show of inspecting the cleanliness of the far wall, then he says, "I'll be back before dawn, and I expect it to be done right this time." He disappears under the portcullis, probably to see his wife, eat a big dinner, and catch some sleep. I think I might hate him.

I point to the bales of hay stacked behind the targets. "We should wash those too," I say, "before the captain invents the job. While we're at it, we might as well wash the portcullis and the archway."

Fernando slumps over with a groan. "Maybe I haven't given enough consideration to the fine life of a tanner."

"Straighten up," I tell him. "Just because you don't see Mandrano or Enrico doesn't mean they don't see you. Assume everything you do is being watched and evaluated."

Fernando grunts and straightens.

I grab my rag and look for something in the yard that hasn't already been senselessly scrubbed.

3

WE'RE allowed to stumble into the barracks just before dawn. Captain Mandrano orders us to stow our three possessions— which we preserved by balancing them on empty, overturned buckets while we washed the yard—and only then will we be allowed into the mess for a meal. After that, we'll be permitted two hours' sleep. Then our real training will begin.

The recruits' room is a squat, low-ceilinged rectangle with earthen walls buttressed by thick wooden beams. Alejandro was right—it's much like a dungeon, with damp, chilly air permeated by the faint scent of rat urine. I console myself with the thought that, after hard days of training in the yard, a damp chill might feel nice.

Three oil lamps hang from the ceiling's center beam. Twelve rickety cots stretch out from the longer walls, six to a side. Beside each cot is a small chest with two drawers. Above each cot is a hanging peg.

I pick the cot nearest the doorway. No one else wants it, for it's bound to be the noisiest. But it also might have the freshest air, and I'd rather be aware of what's going on around me than sleep through it. I hang my brother's plaque, stash my book in one of the drawers, and flip my quilt out over the length of the cot. The latter earns chuckles from several of the recruits, but Fernando gives it an admiring look.

"A girl back home?" he asks.

"Something like that," I say in a tone to discourage further questions. Confessing that the queen herself made it for me is not likely to earn any good will with this group.

Once we've claimed our space and stowed our belongings, we stand at attention by the ends of our cots while Captain Mandrano inspects us. Tomás and Marlo are praised for their hard work and fine example.

He moves down the line. He tells another recruit that his boots are too worn, that he'll have to go barefoot until he is outfitted with a proper pair. When I see the recruit's callused feet, I think that he may be better off without the boots.

Mandrano reaches Lucio. Without a word, he grabs the young man's amphora of wine and dumps it down the floor drain outside the door.

"The amphora is one thing, the wine is another," Mandrano tells Lucio, who is almost as big as he is. "And you're only allowed three things, not four."

"You could have taken my medallion," Lucio says. It's a good luck piece, the image of a Godstone surrounded by a verse from the *Scriptura Sancta* that asks blessings for the bearer.

Mandrano studies it. "No, you're going to need that."

Lucio persists, "I would have drunk the wine and gotten rid of the amphora."

Stop whining, you stupid oaf.

Mandrano's contempt for him is, fortunately, beyond words. He comes to Fernando. "You can't lean your bow against the wall—store it under your bed."

"But that will ruin it," Fernando says.

Mandrano's voice fills the barracks. "Did I ask you for your opinion on weapons? Do you think a recruit knows more about a Guard's weapons than a twenty-year veteran?"

Fernando bites his tongue for once, but it's likely more from exhaustion than anything else. Or maybe he's worried Mandrano will notice the state of his shoes.

Mandrano comes to me last. "That *is* a lovely quilt, recruit," he says.

"Thank you, sir."

"It's the envy of every little girl in Brisadulce. I saw them sitting on the wall today, staring at that blanket and asking their mothers if they could join the Guard so they could have one just like it. Is that what you want, recruit? You want a Guard full of little girls?"

"If they can fight well enough to defend the king, sir."

"Are you talking back to me?"

"No, sir."

"Tuck every bit of that quilt under the mattress, recruit. If I see even the tiniest edge, I will confiscate it and destroy it. Do I make myself clear?"

"Yes, sir."

I do as he asks as quickly as possible. He inspects everything one more time while we sway unsteadily on our feet, our stomachs growling. Finally, *finally*, he gives us leave to seek out a meal.

We tumble from the barracks and into the mess with renewed energy, but we stop short as soon as we arrive. The place is empty.

"What did you expect?" Mandrano says. "You shouldn't have taken so long in the training yard."

Beside me, Fernando whimpers, and I hope with all the hope inside me that Mandrano did not hear.

"The cooks won't arrive to begin breakfast for another half hour," Mandrano says. "You're free until then." All nine of us glower at his back as he leaves.

"Now what?" Fernando says. "I guess we could go back to our room and sleep for a bit."

"I'm not going to risk missing a meal," says one of the others.

"I could thrash Hector now," Lucio suggests hopefully.

I swing my legs over the nearest bench and plop my forearms onto the table. "I'm sleeping right here," I announce. "So I can wake up as soon as the kitchen opens." I let my head drop onto my arms. Lucio can thrash me if he wants, but I'll probably just sleep through it.

I wake to a hand shaking my shoulder, and I jump up, reaching for a sword that isn't there.

"Easy, my lord," says a high voice.

"Just a recruit now," I mumble.

A boy with curly hair backs away from me. I blink at him

to clear sleep from my eyes. It's one of the new pages. Adán or Ando or something like that.

Men are filtering into the mess hall. Easy laughter fills the air, along with the sounds of spoons against bowls and benches scraping the floor. I step away, intending to dart toward the meal line, but the page grabs my arm. "Message from the king," he says. "You're being summoned."

A hush settles over the mess hall. Everyone stares at me. Everyone who isn't glowering, that is. The page holds out a piece of folded parchment.

Alejandro, what have you done?

Captain Mandrano is at my side before I can react, snatching the king's note from my fingertips. "What's this about?" he says.

"How should I know?" I snap. "I haven't read it yet."

Mandrano's glare is as hot as a blacksmith's furnace. My brother Felix used to say that my knives would never be as sharp as my tongue, which was a shame. But seeing Mandrano looking at me with murder in his eyes makes me understand that my sharp tongue will be my downfall unless I learn to control it.

"You can read it, of course," I say.

He turns it over, a tiny square in his large hands, but the seal stops him. "That's His Majesty's mark," he says. "It's addressed to you. Only you can open it."

He means it sincerely, I can tell. The king's seal is sacred to him.

When he hands it back to me, I tear it open at once. *Come*

immediately is all it says in Alejandro's fluid, elegant scrawl.

"Damn it," I say.

A half dozen possibilities run through my mind. Chief among them is an early morning tryst. I used to deliver messages to coordinate his assignations with the court ladies—the errand I hated most. But that can't be it; he ceased all such behavior after marrying Rosaura.

The collective stares of the Royal Guardsmen press in around me, and I realize it doesn't matter why I'm being summoned. Everyone will see this as confirmation that I'm the king's flunky, exempt from the usual standards and behaviors expected of a Royal Guard.

With the seal broken and the message read, Mandrano casts his reservations aside and tears it from my grasp again. "Well, then, *squire*," he says, turning the title into an insult. "You'd better go at once." He stuffs the summons back into my hand and shoves me toward the door. It feels like a permanent dismissal.

The scent of hot, honeyed porridge follows me out of the mess. I'm in the hallway heading toward the palace proper when I hear two Guardsmen talking at my back, loud enough for me to hear.

"Less than a day," the first one retorts with a sneer.

"He hasn't washed out yet."

"He's walking out the door before he's sworn in, and that means that he's washed out. Pay up."

I'm only a Guard recruit because of Alejandro.

And now, because of him, I may have already failed.

4

I can't imagine that the barracks will ever feel as much like home as the palace halls, with their worn cobbled floors and sandstone walls warm with torchlight. I pass the kitchens, waving to the staff. They're doling out leftover bread and cheese from breakfast to children of the palace servants. When the kitchen master sees me, he brandishes a heel of bread at me. My mouth waters, but I keep going.

I stop at a well-lit archway framed with block quartz. Centered in the archway is the desk of Vicenç, Alejandro's mayordomo—though it is empty. A Royal Guard stands rigid beside it, his face stony. In the hallway just before the desk are several plush couches arranged around a thick rug.

This is the waiting area where all visitors to the royal quarters are received. As a page, I spent hours here, waiting to escort guests as needed. But there are no pages here now. Even the mayordomo is absent. But then I notice the Invierne ambassador sitting on one of the couches, his legs elegantly crossed, and I realize their absence is a deliberate snub.

The ambassador stands upon seeing me. He's taller even than Enrico, with pale flowing robes, hair like molten gold, and upturned eyes the color of an emerald cove. Like all Inviernos, he has an ageless quality about him that makes him seem unknowable. He is newly appointed, just since the old king's death, and I don't remember his name. I resist the urge to back away as he gazes at me with haughty disdain.

I hear voices coming toward us from beyond the desk.

A moment later, Vicenç emerges from the shadows, accompanied by General Luz-Manuel, Conde Treviño, and Lord-Commander Enrico. Three of the five Quorum lords.

Lord-Commander Enrico is out of uniform. His civilian clothes are carefully cut to resemble those of the general and conde, though adorned with gold threads and jeweled buttons to emphasize wealth and station.

"Thank you for your reports, gentlemen," Vicenç says. He is a sharp-featured man who probably should not have made the decision to draw attention to his nose with a large, gleaming nose ring. "I assure you the king and queen will announce the birth of their heir very soon." The last statement is the kind of practiced theater that the Invierne ambassador is meant to overhear while he waits. If the royal succession is secure, Joya d'Arena will *not* be weakened by internal conflict. The message is that we are as strong as ever, and now is a very bad time for Invierne to attack.

"I hope they choose a good name for the child. A strong name," says Luz-Manuel. The general is a small, balding man, carried to his position by ambition and wits rather than physical prowess. He proved to have a knack for strategy during the skirmishes with Invierne, and Alejandro's father valued him highly—until one of those skirmishes got King Nicalao killed. Some say the general made a poor decision to flank a smaller, oncoming force, leaving the bulk of his men—including the king—exposed to the larger threat. Luz-Manuel insists the king himself gave the order.

I've always wondered about that.

"Perhaps they'll name him Nicalao," the general continues, "to honor the martial spirit of the late king." I barely refrain from rolling my eyes. What if they have a daughter? Then I realize his comment was merely intended to remind the ambassador of Joya d'Arena's military strength.

Enrico jumps in on cue. "The kingdom will remain stable and strong if— Hector! What in seven hells are you doing here?"

Vicenç appears indifferent to Enrico's unplanned outburst. After serving three kings, it takes an extraordinary event to rouse him beyond bemused detachment. But the conde is openly furious.

Conde Treviño of Basajuan is a self-aggrandizing man who likes to overspend—thus the problem of Lucio, whom he can neither handle nor dispose of without upsetting the boy's wealthy father. He seldom leaves Basajuan to come to the capital, and I'm never glad to see him.

Ignoring the conde's glare, I say to Enrico, "I was summoned, my lord." I hold up my note.

Enrico snatches it from my hands. "What's the meaning of this?"

"I don't know, my lord."

The general reads over his shoulder. He glances at the Invierne ambassador, who suffers the scrutiny unflinchingly. "Let the boy go, Rico," the general says after a moment. "We have other things to discuss."

"And I could use a smoke," Conde Treviño says. "Let's talk about that little problem you're taking care of for me over cigars."

"Of course," the lord-commander says. He takes one last glance over his shoulder at me as the general and conde lead him away.

The gem dangling from Vicenç's nose ring winks in the torchlight as he sits down to work. He pulls reports from a locked drawer and gets busy ticking off numbers and accounts. I approach him. He barely glances up, grumbling, "What now?"

"I've been summoned to the king," I say.

"Well, fetch yourself to him, boy."

"That's not proper procedure, and you know it," I say, unable to keep the anger from my voice. I am not, at the moment, technically a member of the palace household, and security protocol demands that I be escorted.

He doesn't look up a second time. "If I don't have a page or squire to spare at the moment for Ambassador Wafting . . . er, Wind and Thunderstorm"—he makes a vague waving gesture—"then I don't have one for you. So you can stand there all day, or you can obey his summons."

"Yes, my lord," I say, and turn to go.

The Invierne ambassador blocks my way.

"Perhaps I could go with the young gentleman," he says in a fluid, hissing voice. I'm careful not to make eye contact. "It's important that I speak to the king today. It will only take a moment."

"I'm terribly sorry, my lord-ambassador," Vicenç says, "but this is just an errand boy, not even a member of the palace staff. Look at his uniform! I would never embarrass you by sending you without a worthy escort." To me, he says, "Hurry on, boy."

I dash past the Guard, who curls his lip at the sight of my recruit uniform, and I leave the ambassador fuming at my back.

The private quarters of the palace are a maze, deliberately so—no assassin or enemy could make their way in quickly— but I know each turn well, and I head left, past the nobles' quarters, up the stairs, and around the corner to the queen's chambers.

5

DR. Enzo, the royal physician, is leaving as I arrive. He wipes sweat from his forehead, looking preoccupied, but forces a smile when he notices me. A smile from Enzo is never a good sign.

"What's wrong?" I ask.

"I should be asking you that," he says with forced conviviality, his razor-thin mustache twitching. "Aren't you supposed to be in the barracks? I didn't expect to see you again until the inevitable training accident. Did you know that training accidents are disfiguring twenty-three percent of the time?"

"The king summoned me."

"He's in there." He rests a hand on my forearm. "Speak quietly," he says in a low voice. "And do not upset the queen."

I frown. This is a worse sign.

Inside, Queen Rosaura is propped up in her bed, which has been pushed to the glass doors overlooking the balcony. Before her pregnancy, she spent all day outdoors, in the garden or on horseback, and the enforced bed rest has not sat well with her.

One of her maids, Miria, wipes her forehead. When Miria sees me, she makes quick, tiny adjustments to the queen's gown so that it lies flawless and smooth. Miria is about thirty years old, a trusted servant who has lived her whole life in the palace. I don't know much about her except that she is Vicenç's grandniece and she is married to a soldier, either someone in the Royal Guard or the palace watch.

I notice Alejandro last because he sits shadowed in the corner, gazing at his wife. His arms are crossed pensively, and one hand covers his mouth.

"Hector," the queen says, smiling warmly as she always does, as if nothing is wrong. Alejandro jumps from his seat, startled by the sound of her voice.

"Your Majesty," I say, bowing. "You don't look a day older than when last I saw you." My face flames, and I wish I could suck the words back. I never know what to say around women.

But she laughs anyway. "You saw me two days ago!" It's a weak laugh, and I tell myself it's because it was a weak joke. She glances meaningfully at Alejandro. "Shouldn't he be with the recruits?"

"I summoned him," Alejandro says. He strides over and grasps my arm. "Thank you, Hector."

"I just witnessed an interesting bit of theater," I say before I forget. "Vicenç and the Quorum Lords were performing for the new Invierne ambassador, making a big deal about your heir."

Alejandro's face tightens. "Of course," he says, glancing at his wife. "An internal war of succession would provide an opportunity that Invierne's sorcerers could not resist."

Which is why the young king married and set about producing an heir as soon as his father died.

"It's just that . . . well, their performance gave away Her Majesty's exact state of health. Now everyone knows you'll be here together more often than not for the next several days. In the interest of safety, I don't think . . ." Too late, I realize I'm criticizing superior officers—Quorum Lords, no less—not to mention possibly upsetting the queen. I give Rosaura an apologetic look.

But she still smiles. "I told you," Rosaura says to Alejandro. "He's too clever to waste in the Guard."

"Which is why I summoned him," Alejandro replies. "Even if, in this instance, he's probably overthinking things. Allow me to borrow him for a moment, ladies."

Taking my arm, he pulls me to one side of the chamber, where he angles our bodies away from the queen and Miria.

"I need you to go to Puerto Verde for me," Alejandro says in a low voice.

Anger boils up in me, combining with exhaustion and hunger, and I can't stanch the flow of words. "You summoned me away from recruiting day to *run errands* for you? Like when you were courting half the eligible women of the kingdom?"

"I need you, Hector."

"You don't!" My voice is getting too loud. I glance at the

queen, who is exchanging an alarmed look with Miria. In a softer voice, I add, "You have a thousand men you could send to Puerto Verde instead of me."

Alejandro rubs at his chin. He hasn't been shaved yet today.

"I've sent numerous messages through regular channels, and received no response. I had Enrico send members of my Guard, but they also returned without replies. Then, last week I finally sent my own squire. I received word this morning that he was murdered on the highway."

My stomach clenches. "Raúl is dead?"

"I've seen his body."

He was only thirteen, an eager boy and an excellent horseman. I helped to train him. "A squire bearing his king's colors should be safe on the road."

"Precisely," Alejandro says. "He was murdered in his sleep. It was made to look like the work of a bandit, but the wounds were too clean. Too perfect. Nothing was taken. I have to assume foul play. You're the only one I can turn to. You are my army of one."

He has called me that since I came to Brisadulce to be a royal page, for I was the first person he was given charge of who was not merely a servant. "My first command," he used to joke.

"I'm yours to command, now and always." Isn't that what being a Royal Guard is all about anyway? "What do you need me to do?"

He slumps in relief, but he gets straight to the point. "You may remember a certain ring, a ruby as large and red as a cherry, set in a bed of tiny pearls."

"I remember it," I say carefully.

I glance at the queen, who gazes out the window with Miria and carefully pretends not to hear us, and I wonder if we ought to be discussing this in private, for the ruby ring was a gift from Alejandro to the beautiful Isadora de Flurendi, one of his paramours—the lady many assumed would be queen, right up until the moment Alejandro announced his betrothal to Rosaura, her older cousin.

The Flurendi family controls several ports, and Alejandro needed an alliance with one branch or the other to solidify his position. Many times as squire, I helped bring Isadora and Alejandro together, the last time only a few nights before his wedding. Honestly, I had not expected their relationship to end, not even after the marriage to Rosaura. But when the royal couple returned from their honeymoon, they walked around the palace in a state of baffled happiness, genuinely in love with each other. I did not observe what happened between them during the early weeks of their marriage, for I spent that time with my brother Felix, aboard his merchant ship. But I know that the only one more surprised and pleased than me was Alejandro.

The king looks over at his wife, and his gaze softens. "We would very much like to have the one who bears that ring with us at court again. Our many letters have gone unanswered. Rosaura misses her and worries about her deeply."

This doesn't explain the lengths to which he is going to

contact the girl. "May I ask why she is wanted?"

Alejandro's face flushes red, and he looks ashamed, an expression I never thought possible for him until he married Rosaura. "I cannot tell you, not in advance, in case anything should happen. Go and tell her *personally* that the queen and I both request the presence of our beloved cousin at court. Collect your answer from her *personally.*"

"And if I encounter obstacles?"

"Then use your judgment," Alejandro says. "You've always had excellent judgment. I want you to leave without fanfare. And do *not* wear my colors. Just in case . . ." Just in case the squire's murder was no coincidence.

An idea hits me. Maybe there's still a way to preserve my chance at making the Guard. "You must let me take someone along to stand watch while I sleep. Two would be better than one."

"Not possible," Alejandro says. Again, that look of shame.

"If I'm murdered like Raúl, your message will never find its recipient."

Alejandro considers. "You cannot take them with you into her father's fortress, not to deliver our message or to receive her reply. You may tell them nothing."

"Agreed," I say. "I'd like to take two of the other recruits. Their names are Tomás and Marlo—they're experienced soldiers. You will need to authorize their absences. All our absences."

"I'll send two of my Guards with you instead," he says.

"That would draw more attention to your mission," I say.

"And Guards would never follow my lead. Better if we are all recruits."

Also, three absent recruits—two of them Enrico's favorites—will make it harder for the commander to single me out for punishment. He'll be hard-pressed not to take me back.

Alejandro considers. His gaze switches back and forth between Rosaura and me. Finally, he says, "I don't think I could bear to lose you too, Hector." He sounds more tired than I feel, which is saying something.

He'll lose me someday, if I'm to be a Royal Guard. It's what we sign up for. But I hold my tongue on that count.

"I'll draft the order, and you can leave immediately," he says. "Come with me."

"Let him stay and keep us company in your absence, love," the queen says from across the room. She has, of course, been listening the whole time, which doesn't seem to bother Alejandro one bit. Perhaps being truly in love means not having secrets from each other.

Alejandro nods, worry etched on his features. To me, he says, "I'll return in a moment."

I go to the queen.

6

"PREGNANCY suits you, Your Majesty," I say to her, and then wince at yet another awkward compliment.

It's a stretch. She was beautiful when she first became pregnant, glowing like the dawn, as happy as the song of a lark. But as the months have passed, it has worn her down. She still smiles with unrelenting cheer, but there is a heaviness to her, as though she has borne a painful wound for a long time.

"Thank you," she says. "But you are a terrible liar, and I think you always will be."

I start to protest, but she rests her hand on my wrist, and I feel how clammy her skin is. I say lightly, "My incapacity for dishonesty troubles you?"

I mean it as a joke, but she nods. "If you want to serve your king well, then you must learn not to speak at all. It may be the only thing that will prevent you from revealing your secrets."

"I can keep—"

She interrupts my protest with a deep frown.

One does not ignore one's queen's admonition. I pause, and then, finally—wisely, I hope—nod wordlessly.

"Quickly, now, before you go, I must tell you a secret," the queen says. "I must know first if you have the will to stay silent about it, because it could mean your life—or Alejandro's—if you do not."

"I'll not say a word," I promise earnestly.

She removes her hand from my arm and places it on her belly. "My pregnancy does not go well. The child inside me is weak. Doctor Enzo says my own life is in danger."

With those words, something inside me shrivels. Everything suddenly makes sense: Dr. Enzo's false cheer, Alejandro's worry, the queen's pallor. I glance up at Miria, hoping for a denial, but I see my own anguish mirrored in her face.

"Can't Doctor Enzo do something?"

"He is doing everything he can, and it may yet turn out well. Many difficult pregnancies do. But I wish to have my beloved cousin Isadora at my side in this time of distress."

Of the two monarchs, Rosaura is the better strategist—we all know it. She is older than Alejandro, wiser. She understands politics and power and secret deals better than Alejandro ever will. And I am not fool enough to believe they're going to all this trouble to bring in a new lady-in-waiting.

"Brisadulce faces many dangers," she continues. "Invierne is asking for port privileges, maybe to build a navy. They will attack again in force; if not this year, then soon. But Alejandro also faces danger from within. Many who were loyal to his father do not respect him yet."

"They'll learn—"

"Remember what I told you about being a bad liar?"

In this moment, if I could resolve never to speak again, I would. Because I know she is right.

"We don't know who killed Raúl. I'd be surprised if anyone knew *why* my husband is sending messages to Lord Solvaño at the Fortress of Wind. Perhaps disrupting the king, exposing his weaknesses, is motivation enough."

Isadora. The last detail clicks. Alejandro and Rosaura want Isadora at court, because if Rosaura dies, Alejandro can marry her immediately and keep strong ties to the Flurendi family.

Rosaura nods as if she can read my thoughts. "I know Isadora and Alejandro were . . . fond of each other. It would be a good match."

I don't know what to say. The pity on my face must be apparent, because finally her serene composure dies, and her face turns hard, her mouth set with frown lines. "The king must have a wife who can provide an heir. If Alejandro dies without one, I count at least four powerful condes who would claim distant ties to the throne. An ambitious man could even convince himself it was the right thing to do, that fighting for the throne would make the kingdom stronger. There would be civil war. And Invierne stands ready to sweep in and clean up the pieces."

"You think someone has an eye on the throne," I whisper. "Who?"

She smiles and shrugs. "Does it matter? Alejandro will be just as dead."

She suspects someone; I can see it in her face.

"Alejandro has asked you to find her, yes?" she says.

You may remember a certain ring, with a ruby as large and red as a cherry. "Yes."

"When you speak to her, let her know that she is dear to me and that I want her happiness and position assured even before my own."

"I will," I promise. What must it be like, I wonder, to orchestrate a potential marriage for her own husband?

"You may find it harder to deliver your message than Alejandro indicates. My uncle, Isadora's father, is very devout and cloistered, and he rules his keep with iron control. Isadora has not been seen at public functions since she returned home after the royal wedding. There are concerns that her father, having intercepted our letters to her, is keeping her in isolation."

"But why?"

"Perhaps he has convinced himself it is the right thing to do. No one sets out to do evil, you know. We just do our best and let history judge."

History. As if her decisions are already in the past and she is already gone. The lump in my throat vies with the knot in my chest. This situation requires delicacy. It should be attended to by a diplomat, someone wiser in the ways of court and experienced in intrigue.

Rosaura's expression turns sympathetic. "I'm sending

Miria with you. She'll be able to go places in the fortress that you can't go."

"Into the women's quarters," I suggest.

"There and elsewhere," says Miria. Her face is firm with resolve, and I find myself warming to her.

Rosaura says, "She'll meet you outside the city gate after you leave. Agreed?"

"It's not safe," I say. "Squire Raúl—"

"I trust you to protect her," the queen says.

"On my word," I promise again. "But she can't tell anyone, not even her husband, where she's going."

Miria glowers. "My husband would never—"

Rosaura puts up a hand. "He's not accusing anyone of anything, Miria. He's doing his best to keep all of you safe—not from friends, but from the enemies we don't know. Can you obey?"

She hesitates a moment. "I can."

The door adjoining the royal suites opens, and Alejandro strides through, bearing a folded piece of parchment sealed with red wax.

"This should get you what you nee—" His gaze shifts between Rosaura and me. "Everything all right?"

"Of course," the queen says, her usual serenity back in place. "Hector was concerned for our health, but I have assured him that everything is well and going as expected."

She sounds utterly convincing, as bright and genuine as one of her smiles. She's right: I'll never be able to lie so well.

I take the order from Alejandro's outstretched hand. The

wax is still warm. "The sooner I leave," I say, "the sooner I can return."

"I'll pray for you, my friend," Alejandro says, and I can only nod in response.

At least no one suggests that I might not return.

7

IN the training yard, Mandrano is putting the other recruits through basic exercises, seeing how they handle a sword, their fists, an opponent. Their wild swinging and unsteady legs speak to their exhaustion. I suppose I should feel lucky to miss it all, but the clack of wooden weapons, the grunt that follows a hard blow, the smells of sweat and dust call out to me. It's everything I had hoped to be doing.

When Mandrano spots me, he turns deliberately away and makes a show of correcting Fernando's form as the boy skewers a straw dummy with a wooden sword.

I move into his line of sight, and when that doesn't work, I circle around and get right in his face. "A command from His Majesty," I say, holding out the sealed parchment. "He requires my aid, along with that of Tomás and Marlo."

"Why not call upon his own Guard?" Mandrano asks, snatching it from my hand.

"I gather that his Guard is needed for more important duties."

Mandrano tears it open and reads. "This is horse muck."

"What's horse muck?" Commander Enrico strides toward us from the barracks. He pins me with a gaze, and a breeze brings me the lingering sweet-smoke scent of Selvarican cigars.

The other recruits have stopped training or even pretending to train. All attention is now squarely focused on me and the two commanding officers.

Mandrano obediently hands Enrico the parchment. I watch the commander's eyes. He reads it carefully twice, then feigns continued reading while he considers.

"The needs and decisions of kings are beyond the question of the Guard," Mandrano says at last.

"Yes, yes," Enrico says, though I'm not sure he's convinced.

"A Royal Guard obeys his king instantly and without question," Mandrano says louder, speaking now to the recruits more than to his commander.

Enrico glowers, but he nods.

"And we trust that he has an excellent reason for giving us this command," Mandrano adds.

"Indeed we do," Enrico says, and a wicked smile suddenly curves his lips. "Fernando! Lucio!"

The archer and the bully step forward.

"The two of you go pack. His Majesty requires you to run an errand for him with Hector."

"That's not right," I blurt. "It's supposed to be Tomás and Marlo!"

Tomás and Marlo exchange an alarmed glance.

I reach for the note and stop just short of snatching it from Enrico's hand.

He holds it up in a way that's almost taunting. "His Majesty says I'm to send two other recruits. In my judgment, Fernando and Lucio are best qualified to aid you."

I'm fuming, and it must show, because a subtle smile plays across Enrico's lips. He's taking advantage of the opportunity to get rid of three of us at once. I don't care about Lucio—he's only getting what's coming to him—but Fernando doesn't deserve this. His only fault is not knowing anyone to whom Enrico owes a favor. I don't deserve this either.

"Do you have a problem with *my* commands?" Enrico asks.

"No, my lord!" I answer.

"Good," he says. "Mandrano, escort these whelps to their quarters so they can gather their things."

"My lord . . ." I say, and then hesitate.

Enrico watches me like a hangman doling out rope to his victim. "Yes, princess?"

"It should only take a few days to get there and back. We'll return to our training immediately after."

Enrico smiles. "There is no mention here of how long this . . . *errand* will take. We can't assume you'll return before the evaluation is complete. It's possible you'll miss so much training that you won't be able to catch up with everyone. We'll have to decide what to do with you when you return. Understood?"

My heart sinks. "By my king's command, my lord," I say.

"Fernando! Lucio!" Enrico snaps. "Clear the barracks of all your things *now*."

As they rush to comply, I realize assassins along the highway are now the least of my worries. Based on the looks Fernando and Lucio are throwing over their shoulders at me, they'll team up to murder me themselves.

"You too, princess," Mandrano says, though the barb seems halfhearted. He's looking up at Enrico, a puzzled expression on his face. "Go get that pretty dress off your cot and pack up."

8

THE walk to the stables is fraught with silent, seething anger. "What in seven hells is going on?" Lucio rages as soon as we are out of earshot.

"I've told you everything I can," I say. "The king is sending us as couriers to Puerto Verde. We'll come back as soon as we're done."

"I don't care if you're kissing camels to get the favors you get," he says. "But if you muck up my one chance to get into the Guard—"

"You think this is a *favor*?" I fume. "You think I asked for this?"

"If it gets you out of training with—"

"Calm down," Fernando says. "We're doing something for the king. That's why we want to be in the Guard, right, so we can do things for the king?"

He addresses Lucio, but his eyes are on me.

"You heard Enrico," Lucio says. "He's going to throw us out like so much trash when we get back."

"But it's King Alejandro's Guard, right?" Fernando says, his eyes still fixed on me. He's trying to parse his own chances.

"So I've heard," I say.

"It's the *king's* Royal Guard," Lucio says. "Not Alejandro's. It was his father's before, and it'll belong to whomever comes after."

"We won't have to worry about that for a long time," I say.

"It could be tomorrow or the day after," Lucio says. "Everyone knows Alejandro would rather chase skirts than chase an enemy. The one time he fought Invierne, he nearly died of fright. Remember? The day King Nicalao took an arrow? They say Alejandro panicked. Cried like a—"

I smash my fist into Lucio's face. He loses his balance and tumbles into a stall filled with straw. I jump on top of him and throw jabs at his face as fast and hard as I can.

His arms are longer than mine. He absorbs my blows as if they're nothing while groping for my neck. His thumbs press into my windpipe. I grip the side of his skull and jam my thumbs into his eyes.

Stars swim in my vision, but I have the satisfaction of feeling him twist and buck beneath me, of hearing him squeal in pain.

Something grabs my collar and yanks me off of him. Lucio starts to launch himself after me, but a steel-toed boot pins his chest to the ground.

"Hector! What in the king's name is going on here?" It's Felipe, the stable master, and we boys have proven no match for the man who wrangles war chargers all day.

My head swims, and the edges of my vision blur. My throat convulses, trying to suck in air. Felipe knows me well. He'll assume Lucio is in the wrong, and he'll likely call the palace watch to have him arrested.

Finally, I'm able to force out the words: "Nothing! It's fine . . . it's over."

Lucio glares at me, angry but confused.

"We had a disagreement," I add, rubbing my throat. Breathing comes easier now, but I'm going to have nasty bruises. "We worked it out."

"Is that true?" the stable master says.

Lucio looks at me, then glances at Fernando, who stands silently off to the side, his face a careful blank. "We worked it out," he mutters.

Without giving details, I explain that we're on an errand for the king. I ask for Blaze, who was my horse when I was squire, but he was stolen when Raúl was murdered. Instead I end up with Sosimo, a chestnut gelding with a strong temperament and fine bones, who can set the pace for the two other mounts.

Soon we are on our way, our horses swishing their tails against the tiny sand flies that always cloud the air for a few weeks after the rainy season. The day is hot, and both the ocean to our right and the desert to our left are blindingly bright. Neither Fernando nor Lucio say a word to me. Which suits my mood fine, since I've got nothing to say back.

We are well into the desert before Miria joins us. She is

dressed in rough-spun wool, like a desert nomad. She sits astride a dun mare, just off the road.

"Where are you headed?" she calls.

"Puerto Verde," I reply.

"May I travel with you? The roads are not safe for a woman alone."

"Suit yourself," I answer.

Miria introduces herself by name, but does not mention that she works at the palace. Lucio and Fernando size her up appreciatively; she's attractive enough, I suppose, with pretty eyes and the healthy, well-fed look of a merchant or higher-class servant. But she is old enough to be our aunt, and after a few minutes, Lucio ignores her. Fernando tries a few jokes, but she doesn't respond, and soon we are all traveling in silence.

The first day's journey takes us to a way station consisting of a long feed trough and a tying post for horses and camels, several palm-thatch lean-tos, and a deep well. Miria takes one of the lean-tos, and the rest of us set up just outside, where we have a good view of the highway. After tending our mounts, we share a small, silent meal. As the sun dips into the sea, casting the desert sand in fiery red, I tell Fernando to take the first watch.

"Shout if you see anything unusual," I tell him. "Anything at all."

"If I see an extra serving of dinner, I'm keeping it for myself," he says.

My plan is to stay awake and watch him keep watch, but

the lack of sleep from the night before catches up with me.

I'm jerked from sleep by a shout. The twang of a bow. A thump nearby.

By the time I'm on my feet, sword in hand, there's a body lying at my feet.

9

FERNANDO'S arrow is buried deep in a man's chest. A perfect shot.

The dead man is unkempt and rough looking, the kind of man you wouldn't glance at twice if he were a field hand or part of a deck crew. Good chance he was one or the other for most of his life. White scars, cold in the moonlight, welt along the knuckles that still grip the knife he carries; he probably brawled for money on the side. The blade he clutches is short and sharp, for slitting swiftly and quietly.

"He studied us," Fernando says. "Then he moved so fast. I didn't know what to do, and I just . . ."

"Tell me," I say.

"He stepped into the glow of the firelight, quietly, and I was . . . tired. . . . I thought maybe I was dreaming. He studied us all, even me—he must have thought I was asleep—then drew the knife—"

"You did the right thing," I say quickly. "This man was sent to kill us."

"What?" Lucio says.

"He was matching our descriptions. Someone told him we were coming this way."

I let the information sink in, then I add, "We may still be in danger. Fernando, keep that bow ready. You and Lucio go check the road. See if our assassin has company. If he does, try to take him alive so we can question him. Now go!"

It must be the rush of blood in their veins, because they jump to obey. I dash to the nearby lean-to and shake Miria awake. She is on her feet instantly, and I explain as we head back to the campsite.

"Quick, help me search him," I whisper. "He may carry something we would not want the others to see."

She does not flinch from the blood as she goes through his jacket, checking the pockets and linings and seams, while I check his trousers, then pull off his boots. Miria and I exchange a glance and both shake our heads. He carries nothing that would identify him.

This may be our only chance to talk, so I blurt, "Is Rosaura really dying?"

Miria glances around to make sure we are truly alone. "Dr. Enzo thinks it likely."

She is only confirming what I already knew, but the sadness inside me is suddenly a physical pain. "And Isadora . . ."

"The women are first cousins," she says. "And close friends. I'm not sure why the king ultimately chose Rosaura, but he loved Isadora first."

Footsteps startle us. Fernando and Lucio return with a horse.

"This is all we found," Lucio says.

I leap up, hoping the horse will be Blaze, proof that this is the same man who killed Raúl, but we have no such luck; the beast is as unidentifiable as its late owner. Fernando can't take his eyes off the assassin's body. I hope it is the moonlight giving the boy a sickly sallowness, that he will not vomit up his meager dinner. Lucio's jaw is set, grim and serious, when he sees the pockets turned out and the seams ripped open.

I make up my mind.

"There is more I must tell you," I say. "But first, tie the horse to the post, as if he were staying here overnight. Then pack up your gear."

They nod and go to it.

"Here, help me," I say, rolling the body over. Miria braces the body up, and I snap the arrow and remove the pieces. I throw them down the well, where they won't be found.

Fernando and Lucio return a moment later. "What's going on here?" Lucio demands.

"I carry a secret message from the king to someone in the Fortress of Wind," I say.

"That's Lord Solvaño de Flurendi's castle," Lucio says.

"Yes. The king has sent messages through official channels, including his Guards, but has received no response. So he sent someone he personally trusted—his squire—who was murdered."

"That's why he came to you," Lucio says. "You're his last

resort. Must be a damned important message."

Lucio is smarter than I've been giving him credit for. Fernando remains silent.

"There is one other thing you must know." I work as I talk, saddling my own horse, cinching up Rosaura's quilt onto the back like a bedroll. "Miria is one of the queen's servants."

"My lady," Lucio says with a slight bow. He's had some practice.

Fernando grows paler.

"I'm just a servant," Miria says. "Not a lady." She glares at me. "His Majesty told you not to tell them anything."

"He also said to use my judgment. I don't want them endangering themselves or our mission through ignorance."

She pauses, then says, "Fair enough."

I help saddle her horse.

"Are we just going to leave him here?" Fernando says, still staring at the body.

"A victim of robbery," I say. "Robberies are not unheard of at these way stations. Let's get rid of any sign we passed this way. With luck, whoever hired him won't find out what happened for some time."

We're back on the road an hour before dawn, but I can't imagine any of us wanting to sleep. Wind has swept sand onto the road, which muffles the steps of our horses. In the dark, an assassin could sneak up on us easily.

The silence is finally broken by Fernando, just as the eastern sky is turning from black to blue. "I've never killed anyone before."

"You did the right thing," Miria says swiftly.

"It was a quick decision and an accurate shot," I say. "You did well."

Another silence. Then Lucio speaks. "I've killed someone."

I'm not surprised. I give him what I hope is an encouraging look.

"When I was six years old."

Now I'm surprised.

"I was at my aunt's wedding. My cousin, who was only four, was chosen over me to throw petals along the bridal walk. He got a special suit of clothes made, and at the wedding, he danced with the bride, even had a sip of wine. It all seems so stupid now, but I remember shoving him. His head hit the corner of a table. It cracked his skull open. He bled all over my aunt's wedding *terno*."

My stomach sinks.

"I brought shame on the whole family. My mother shunned me. My father fostered me in other houses."

"I'm sorry," Miria says. "That must have been very hard for you."

"If I don't make the Guard, I don't know where I'll end up."

"You'll make it," I tell him, though I'm not sure I believe it.

The desert air is turning hot with daylight before Lucio speaks again.

"Have you ever killed anyone, Hector?"

"Not exactly," I say. It's not something I like to talk about, but now I owe Lucio a story. "I failed to save a man's life last summer. We were aloft in the rigging of my brother's ship. A rope snapped and a block came loose—it hit Juan in the head and he fell into the sea."

There had been so much blood, a crimson arc of it, trailing him as he slipped off the tilting spar and dropped unconscious into the waves.

"On the next roll of the ship I leapt from the mast into the water, but the sails had already carried us away. I swam as fast as I could. He was sinking. . . . I got to him, eventually, and held his head above the water until they could send a boat back to pick us up. But I didn't get there fast enough. He never regained consciousness, and he died the next day. My brother said the water killed him, not the blow to the head."

Fernando still has said nothing. Lucio reaches over and clasps his shoulder.

"Cheer up," he says. "You killed one man who deserved it and saved four lives. That makes you better than Hector and me combined. If any of us makes it into the Guard now, it should be you."

Fernando's smile is weak, but grateful. For the first time, I feel a spark of gladness that Enrico chose these two to send with me.

10

WE stand watch every night, but no one else comes after us, and we reach Puerto Verde three days later. It's a port city, surrounded on three sides by sandstone cliffs. The bay is a deep emerald green, and filled with merchant ships, fishing trawlers, even a few pleasure barges. The Fortress of Wind sits atop a spur of rock that juts out into the bay. We see its distant outline as we enter the city.

"Have you heard the stories?" Lucio asks.

"About Princess Brindé?" Miria says. "She was locked in the tower by her father, until a brave sea captain climbed the wall to rescue her."

Seawater froths at the base of the tower, spouting into the air with each pounding wave. Climbing it would be impossible.

"I doubt it's true," I say, reaching into my saddlebag. "There is no Princess Brindé in the historical record." I pull out the book on the architecture of Joya d'Arena that was a gift from my mother—just far enough to give them a peek at the cover.

"According to this, the original tower was a lighthouse, used to warn ships at night. Inviernos stormed the lighthouse and extinguished it, and Admiral Hugano lost his entire fleet on the rocks. That's when the fortress was built to protect the lighthouse."

"But it's not a lighthouse anymore," Fernando says.

"No," I say. "The queen's great-grandfather dredged the port and built a jetty, which made him a very rich man. This castle stayed in the family, though."

Lucio adds, "Lord Solvaño charges a small berth fee to ships in port. All captains are required to use local crew to load and unload cargo, and he takes a small tax. It's how he maintains his wealth."

I give Lucio a sharp look. I hadn't known that.

It takes an hour to navigate the warren of docks and warehouses that makes up Puerto Verde and reach the other side. Up close, the Fortress of Wind is wholly at odds with the wealthy reputation of its keeper. It seems to be crumbling under its own weight and is all the more imposing for its overgrown walls and wild gardens and tattered banners. The front gate is rusted orange and smothered with purple bougainvillea. Two sentries regard us coldly, but I show them the king's seal, and they wave us through.

Then we are forced to wait in a cold hall, where dust motes gray the air and a nearby hearth sits ashy and dead. Finally, Lord Solvaño comes to receive us.

I've seen him many times before at court. He's a man who seems to simultaneously grow larger and smaller, swelling in girth but shrinking in sympathy and character until only anger remains.

He crosses his arms and glares. "What are you doing here?"

Solvaño does not have a reputation for delicate diplomacy.

"We have a message for your daughter from the king," I say, handing him a missive with Alejandro's orders—but not the message itself. "Could we see the lady Isadora, please? We'll deliver His Majesty's message, take her reply, and be on our way."

"She's not here," he says. He holds the missive as if it was a jellyfish, a repulsive thing that might sting him.

"Where did she go?" I ask. "Our orders are to deliver the king's message to its recipient, wherever she may be. "

Lord Solvaño frowns. "I cannot tell you."

"Why not? The king will order a search." I don't know if he will or not, and the slight deception does not sit well. I shift uncomfortably, imagining Rosaura's disapproving look.

"No, no," he insists. His eyes twitch like a pair of dice coming to rest. "She asked me not to tell."

"So you have a way of communicating with her, then?"

"Of course I do."

"Then tell her that the king's messengers await, and she will come to us."

"I'll send her the message," he says. "I'll convey her reply directly to the palace at Brisadulce. *If* she replies, that is. She has always been disrespectful and irresponsible."

The last statement is the first he's said that he actually believes, but it does not at all fit with my impression of the warm, intelligent woman with whom I arranged correspondences and meetings for so many months.

"We'll wait here until she responds," I insist.

"You don't want to do that," he says with a polite smile. "My daughter is not worth the king's trouble."

"It's not for me to decide who is, or is not, worth His Majesty's trouble. We're happy to wait." And I can't help adding, "We've heard such nice things about the lovely hospitality of the Fortress of Wind."

"It will be several days before I can get a message to her. I'd hate to waste your time."

"Our time is the king's to waste, and he asked us to personally collect her reply. We'll stay until we hear from her. Of course, if it would be faster for us to go to Isadora ourselves, we're happy to do so."

His face goes cold and hard. "I'll have my staff find rooms for you."

"Thank you," I say. I wait until he's turning away, and then, because I wish to discomfit him further, I reach inside my jacket and pull forth the book. "Oh, Lord Solvaño, one other thing."

"I'm at your service," he snaps impatiently.

I hold up the book. "I've a personal interest in architecture, and I recently read Master Jinto's seminal paper on the Fortress of Wind. I'd consider it a great favor if I could tour the original tower."

It also might give me access to parts of the fortress I wouldn't otherwise have.

He hesitates a breath too long. "Of course," he says. "My staff will show you whatever you wish. You!" He indicates a young serving woman with a lift of his chin. "See to our guests."

She flinches away from him, almost imperceptibly. "Yes, my lord." Her skin is sallow, and a large bruise purples her forearm.

The rest of Solvaño's staff follows as he sweeps from the hall. The servant girl stares after him. Is she meant to spy on us?

Gently, Miria asks her, "Could I have mint tea, please? Double-steeped?"

The servant gives her a clumsy but grateful curtsy, then scurries away. Miria has given us a chance to talk privately.

The four of us bend our heads together.

"He's lying," Miria whispers.

"Agreed," I say. "Wherever Isadora is, she is not far. Her father does not strike me as a man who would let her out of his sight. I'm surprised he allowed her to come to court."

"He sent her to win King Alejandro's hand," Miria says. "He instructed her to do whatever necessary to become queen."

"I didn't know that." Poor Isadora. My mother always said that forced marriages are a tragedy—no one should have to marry someone they don't love. Though, looking back, I'm certain Isadora held *some* kind of affection for Alejandro.

"So what do we do?" Lucio asks.

I hesitate, feeling unsure. This is where we could use a statesman. A tried-and-true commander.

"I can talk to the servants," Miria says. "See if they know anything. Servants are more likely to talk to other servants."

"Yes, good idea," I say, relieved to have any kind of suggestion at all. "Lucio," I say. "Wander the docks and the market, ask for stories about the tower." Lucio is from distant, rural Basajuan and will seem like the perfect yokel to these people. They may tell him things they wouldn't tell the rest of us.

"I'm to play the ignorant outlander, yes?" he says.

A grin sneaks onto my face before I can stop it.

"I suppose I have no choice but to indulge in a flagon of wine. To complete the part."

"I'm glad you're willing to make such sacrifices for your king," I say, and he nods solemnly.

"Fernando?"

He jumps as if he's been shot with an arrow.

Perhaps Fernando is still not over killing a man. If so, I need to distract him. "We must be prepared," I say. "You've proven yourself an able guard, so I need you to stick with me or Miria, watch our backs at all times. Can you do that?"

I'm not sure it's the right thing to do, but during the summer I crewed on my brother's ship, Felix's response every time I showed even a hint of nervousness or hesitation was to keep me busy.

"Yeah, I can do that," Fernando says. The deep breath he

takes seems like his first in many long days.

"You don't care if something happens to *me*?" Lucio says.

I open my mouth to say something scathing, but wisdom, for once, wins out. "I think that, of all of us, you are most able to take care of yourself."

"Oh." Anger plays across his features, warring with acceptance. Acceptance wins. He puts a hand to the dagger at his belt, and his features harden with determination.

Miria's expression is harder to read, but I feel as if she's watching, judging. She'll report back every tiny detail of this trip. It might even be the real reason she is here. But I can't think about that too much, not until after we find Isadora.

The serving girl returns and apologizes, explaining that it's not the right season for mint, but the cook will be out in a moment to personally offer Miria her choice of spices. "Your rooms will be ready soon after," she assures us.

"Thank you," I say.

"How long do you think you'll be in Puerto Verde?" she asks with a twitchy smile. I can't tell if her artlessness is meant to suss out information or if it's a genuine attempt at conversation.

"As long as it takes," I say with a forced smile of my own.

"Oh. But what if the lady never responds? You can't stay here forever! I mean, you could I suppose, but . . ."

"As long as it takes," Lucio repeats, his voice firm, and the girl's mouth slams closed.

11

ON the afternoon of our second day, the four of us squeeze into my room. It's a tiny chamber with threadbare furnishings and a single window overlooking the sea. Though the day is too warm, a fire roars in the small hearth. I hope the crackle and spit of wood will confound eavesdroppers—as well as make it unbearably warm for anyone hiding near the chimney, where the wall is thick enough to conceal a listening cubby.

"How go your inquiries?" I ask Miria, keeping my voice low.

"Not well," she admits. "I think I've spoken with every cook, scullery maid, manservant, and washing woman in the house, and they are all too afraid to say anything directly." She pauses. "There is something odd, though. . . ."

"Yes?"

"All of Isadora's personal servants were released from service."

I frown. When my grandmother died, her personal attendants were reassigned rather than released. Mamá said that as long we could afford to keep them, there was no reason to lose skilled, loyal help. "Do you think Isadora is . . . dead?"

She shakes her head. "The servants speak of her as though she lives, though they refuse to give details. And another thing: Have you seen the boy in the kitchen who is missing a couple fingers?"

I nod. "Not an unusual injury for the kitchens."

"It was no accident," Miria says. "Lord Solvaño caught him stealing a piece of cake during a Deliverance Day feast. He grabbed the cake knife and cut off the boy's fingers right there."

Fernando gasps.

"That's . . . excessive," I say.

"Solvaño said he would have cut off his whole hand to mark him as a thief, but the cake knife was not large or sharp enough to get through the boy's wrist."

I suppress a shudder.

"Well, that explains what I've been hearing down on the docks," Lucio says.

"Oh?"

"Half the people I talk to worship him like a god. He punishes criminals brutally and swiftly. They believe it successfully discourages crime."

"The other half?" I press.

"They refuse to talk about him at all. I think . . . I think they might be terrified of him."

"Did anyone say anything about Isadora?" Fernando asks.

"No. Although word is out that Solvaño has ordered extra

supplies to host four royal envoys. He's been bragging about it, apparently."

"Envoys?" I laugh.

"You don't consider us envoys?" Miria says to me sharply.

Fernando and Lucio look to me for a reaction, so I'm quick to clarify. "I'm just surprised he's bragging about hosting *us*. He could not have greeted us less warmly."

"According to the wine merchant, he boasted about how much it was costing him to provide for his important guests. To be honest, I didn't even realize the merchant was talking about us at first," Lucio says.

"You weren't buying wine, were you?" I ask, suddenly on alert.

"I don't have any money, so I tried to barter for it," Lucio admits.

I grab him by the collar, ready to go after him like I did in the stable. "I thought you were *joking* earlier. If you drink on duty, so help me God, you will never carry a sword in Alejandro's service. If we'd been too drunk to set watch on the road the other night—if Fernando had been too tipsy to hit his target—we'd all be dead."

He puts up his hands and leans back, but there is no place for him to go except into the fireplace. "I didn't mean anything by it," he says. "I didn't—"

"I mean *everything* by it," I say. I refuse to end up dead, or even cut from the Guard, because some eighteen-year-old man-boy is in his cups. "A Guardsman gets regular leave, a couple days a month. If you want to spend every minute of that leave drunk, I'll buy your wine for you. But never, ever touch a drop when you're on duty. And until we get back to Brisadulce, you're on duty *every single minute*. Do I make myself clear?"

He is silent a long moment. A muscle in his cheek twitches. Then he says, "I didn't drink any. I wanted to. But I . . ." He looks down. Scuffs his boot against the rug. "I poured it over the side of the dock."

"Oh." I'm not sure what to say. He's probably lying about pouring out the wine. But what if he's not? Maybe, just maybe, he wants to make it in the Guard as much as I do.

Again, I notice Miria watching me. "Do you have something to say?" I ask.

She shakes her head.

Lucio straightens his collar and tugs down the hem of his shirt. "It was wine from *your* family the merchant was selling. A shipload just arrived from Ventierra with an early harvest red."

"My brother's ship," I say. "He is—*was*—going to come visit me when they made port in Brisadulce."

I'm thinking about whether I should try to meet him here in Puerto Verde when Miria says, a bit archly, "What progress have *you* made?"

I sigh. "Well, I've ruined a priceless book with bad drawings." I lean against the bedpost, thumbing through the book. "The mayordomo took me on an impossibly quick tour of the fortress. I had to demand more time so I could make sketches."

"He's catalogued every room in the tower," Fernando says in a pained voice. He patiently kept watch while I sketched.

I shake my head. "If they have something to hide, it's not in the tower. The mayordomo made a point of showing me all twelve chambers, which they now use for storage. They're cold and damp from the ocean, crusted with sea salt. Some of the walls are badly cracked. The whole place is gloomy and awful; only five chambers even have windows."

"Six windows," Lucio says.

"I'm sure it's five," I say.

He's looking over my shoulder at the sketches. "Those drawings aren't that bad."

"The author made these." I flip the pages and start showing him the sketches in the margins and in back. "These are mine."

Lucio winces. "Are you sure that's a room?" he says. "It looks like a wagon."

"From this angle," Fernando says, cocking his head. "It's kind of pretty. Like a flower."

"Very funny, both of you. What I lack in talent, I make up for in thoroughness. I measured each room by step, took notes of all the details. We didn't see anything suspicious."

Miria leans forward. "If there's an extra room, it's well hidden."

Lucio nods. "There are definitely six windows in the tower."

"How did you count six?" I ask Lucio.

"From the docks, looking up. I was trying to imagine the

story." He shifts on his feet, looking shamefaced. "About the rescue of the princess."

For the first time in days, I feel a sense of hope. "If we rescue this princess," I say, "it'll be because of you."

Lucio startles at the praise, but his expression goes quickly blank.

"A hidden room," Miria muses, tapping her forefinger to her lip.

"She has to be there. She *has* to be. If we figure out which one, maybe we can get a message to her through the window."

"Let's all go for a walk," Fernando suggests cheerfully.

Given Solvaño's tremendous wealth, it's a wonder the Fortress of Wind is in such disrepair. We stroll across crumbling ramparts, wade through overgrown gardens, clamber over the barnacle-encrusted foundation. Everywhere we go, someone watches us—usually a guard, sometimes a servant—always at a discreet distance.

We're able to match a few windows with my sketches, but by afternoon, we reluctantly agree that we won't get a good enough view without some distance from the tower. So we claim a desire to do some shopping, and head down to the market wharf.

We pretend to browse and sightsee, gradually navigating the maze of docks that twists through the harbor like tree roots. Lucio leads us down an empty jetty that takes us as close to the tower as possible—which is not very close at all. We look up, shading our eyes as the afternoon sun washes the tower in fiery orange, and we finally find what we're looking for.

No wonder it was impossible to spot from a nearer vantage, for it is small and inset—barely wide enough for an arm to fit through. It lies three-quarters of the way up the tower and faces directly west. It's just low enough to catch some ocean spray, which makes the wall too slick to climb.

But the window is open.

"Think she'd hear us if we shouted?" Lucio says.

"That high up? With that surf?" The waves pound at the foundation, then retreat to swirl dark and deep. "If we yelled loud enough, it would bring everyone in the fortress down on us." The wind whips around us, pulling at our hair and clothes.

"Fernando," I say.

"Yes?" He is looking around for danger, as he has been since I tasked him with watching my back. This jetty seems abandoned; the planking is worn and missing in places, and what's left is covered in gull droppings. But I'm glad he's on the alert.

"You won the king's archery contest," I remind him.

"True, my lo—" He stops short of calling me "lord." He's done that a couple of times now.

I point to the window on the tower. "Anyone can put an arrow through a man at short range. I need you to put an arrow through that window."

He sizes up the distance, the target, and the wind, and doubt flows across his face. "We're not on solid ground. And this is a terrible angle. Maybe if I got directly in front of it? But that would mean getting into a boat, which would be even less stable. . . . No, this is an almost impossible shot. Even for the best archer in the kingdom."

"I'm looking at the best archer in the kingdom," I say. "And I believe that you can make it."

"You want to put a note on the shaft and send it through the window," he says.

"Exactly." He watches incredulously as I take out my charcoal stick and write in my book: *Isadora, if you need aid, give us a sign.—The king's envoys.*

I tear the page out and hand it to Fernando, who folds it around the shaft and ties it with a piece of spare bowstring. "The added weight and drag of the note *does* make this an impossible shot," he mutters.

"You can do it," Lucio says.

Fernando draws, sights, releases. The wind catches it and carries it out to the ocean.

The next one bounces off the stone wall and falls into the swirling waves below.

So it goes, shot after shot. I have just torn another page out of the book when the wind whips it from my hands and carries it into the water. I am ruining my mother's priceless gift, and possibly for nothing.

"This is my last arrow," Fernando says.

He waits until he feels a dead spot in the wind. I hold my breath. He lets fly. This time the arrow looks as if it will miss, but it curves toward the narrow slit at the last second, hits the edge, and bounces inside.

We break out into cheering. "I can't believe you made it," Lucio says, and his huge grin makes him seem positively friendly and pleasant.

"You said I could!" Fernando replies.

"I was lying to make you feel better."

Miria is looking back toward the busy docks and the shoreline. "I hope no one heard us," she says. "Or saw us shooting at the tower."

I frown. "I think it's safe to assume that word of our actions will reach Lord Solvaño within the day. As soon as we hear from Isadora, we'll have to move fast."

And then we wait, a long time, with no reaction, no response.

The sun grows too hot. Lucio sweats like a beast, which I realize might be more from dumping his wine than the heat. Fernando polishes his bow with a rag, muttering about damage from saltwater spray.

"It was a good plan," Miria says eventually. "But if she's hidden somewhere else, if she's not in that room . . ."

"She *has* to be there," Fernando says, with all the fervor of someone who can't bear to waste a perfect shot.

"Maybe she needs something write with," Lucio says.

"We'll wait," I say.

Suddenly, an arrow flies out the window. The sunlight glints off something bulky as it drops, spinning end over end and hitting the wall twice before taking a final bounce into the sea.

I whip off my shirt and plunge into the cold waves. Fernando yells at my back—something about rocks and surf. I dive into an oncoming wave and come up the other side. Treading water, I try to figure out where the arrow went in and where the waves might have taken it next. My heart sinks as I realize there is only one place to go—the sharp rocks at the base of the tower, where the waves would pound my bones to sand.

Just then something bobs to the surface, mere yards ahead of me. I stroke forward as a wave crashes over my head. I come up, sputtering, but so does the arrow. I grab for it. It's heavier than I expect, because it's attached to a water skin that has been filled with air and stoppered. Smart girl!

I swim back toward the jetty—at a diagonal to keep the waves from pushing me under—all while holding tight to my prize.

"What is it?" Lucio yells. He and Fernando grab my arms and help me roll up onto the wood planking.

I get to my feet and bend over, breathing hard for a moment. Water runs off me as I hold up the arrow and its attached water skin. Tied to the shaft is a familiar ring, one I have seen many times. It has a ruby as large and red as a cherry, in a setting of tiny pearls.

Lifting my head up toward the window, I say, "Hang on, Isadora. We're coming."

12

"WE make our move tonight," I tell everyone as we head back to the tower. "They'll have noticed our outing today."

"Not to mention your obsessive cataloguing of the tower," Fernando grumbles.

I nod. "We can't give Lord Solvaño the opportunity to smuggle her away."

"This might require force," Lucio says, in his most menacing voice. I'm glad he's on our side.

"Or bribes," Miria says. "It's easier to bribe a fearful servant than a happy one. I think I know where to start."

"We'll be ready for both, if needed."

"Will we just walk out the front door with her?" Fernando asks. "If Solvaño has her locked up, he has a reason. He'll use his guards to stop us."

"We're going to need a lot of bribes," Lucio says.

"When we get her out of the tower, we'll sneak her along the ramparts to the wall on the harbor side. That's only a fifteen-foot drop."

"You can't drop her that far!" Miria says.

"We'll lower her with a rope. We'll have the horses there, with an extra mount for her, and then we'll ride out of the city and back to Brisadulce. We'll be there before Lord Solvaño knows we're gone."

Everyone thinks about this for a minute.

"I don't have any better ideas," Fernando says.

"It could work," Lucio says.

"It could work if we had enough money on hand to bribe servants and guards, buy rope and other supplies, and purchase a horse," Miria says. "That will cost us a small fortune that we don't have."

I think of the plaque Aracely gave me, the one that would give me a chance to start over again if I don't make the Guard.

"I have a small fortune," I say.

Three sets of eyebrows raise, but no one doubts me.

Buying things with jewels instead of coin is problematic; everyone thinks you're a criminal, and everyone overcharges. Nevertheless, by sunset we have everything set. Fernando and Lucio wait below the wall with five horses and supplies. I wait in my room, a coiled rope inside my shirt, a loose cloak over my shoulders. I trace the letters of my now-ruined plaque. *Harsh winds, rough seas, still hearts.*

Miria arrives with a nervous serving girl, the awkward spy who waited on us the first day. We have paid her enough money that she can leave the city and find work elsewhere.

Miria has promised her an interview at the royal palace if our plan succeeds.

"Thank you for helping us," I say.

"She was always nice to me. It's not right, what he did" is her answer.

"What *did* he do?" I ask.

"You'll see soon enough, if you're successful." She turns away. "If you're not, it's my life if I tell."

Though I press her, she will not say more.

With the servant girl in the lead, we hurry through the halls and into the tower. Our bribes have made the place eerily silent. There is only the crackling of our torches, the wind whistling against cracked mortar, and the surf pounding relentlessly below. Still, I listen hard for footsteps or the creak of armor. We could not possibly bribe the entire household, and those we did bribe can't risk being absent from their posts for long.

We wind up the tower stairs and into a storage room. I remember sketching this one. During the day, light filters in as sickly green, for the glass of the window is fogged over with brine and gull droppings.

The servant girl pushes aside an empty crate, revealing a door. No, it's more like a hatch, which we will have to stoop to pass.

"Wait until I leave before you use it," she says. "I mean to be far away."

"Of course," I say. "And thank you."

She turns to go, but Miria grabs her arm. "Wait. Who

among Solvaño's staff knows about this place and who is kept here?"

"I don't know. Not many." The girl tries to jerk her arm away.

"Give me your best guess," Miria orders.

"The guard captain, me, the kitchen master. Only those of us who keep watch or prepare and bring food. And none of us are allowed to go inside. My orders were to open the door, slide the food tray inside, and close it right away. Now please let me go."

"How long until she is missed?" I ask.

"You have until morning." With that, she wrenches away her arm and slips from the room.

"I hope she makes it to Brisadulce," Miria says, staring after her.

"I hope we do too." I lift the bar and swing open the hatch, revealing a dark, damp space. Fetid air washes my face. A rat scurries out of the corner and zips past our feet.

"Isadora?" I whisper.

Chains rattle. "Hector?" comes a weak, muffled reply. "Is that you?"

My eyes adjust to the dark, and I see her for the first time.

"Oh, my dear child," Miria says, rushing forward.

Isadora is huge with pregnancy. A tattered cloth wraps her face. She sits in a vile-smelling puddle, and she is manacled by the ankles to the wall. Her ankles have swollen around the manacles, like soft dough being squeezed. One bleeds badly. From when she stretched to reach the window, I realize with a sinking heart.

"My God," I say, striding toward her. The cruelty of it all is too much to think on. I lift the pommel of my dagger above the chain, eager to pound at something.

"The key is over there," she says, pointing to a ledge beside the door. "He taunts me by leaving it just out of reach."

I grab it and unlock her manacles. They come away from her ankles with a wet sucking sound, but Isadora does not cry out. Miria helps her to her feet.

"We can't lower her over the wall," Miria says.

"I'm strong enough," I protest. "I can—"

Miria gives me a wilting glare. "It's not the weight of pregnancy. It's her health. My lady, can you walk?"

"Show me this wall and I'll leap, just to be done with it," Isadora replies acidly.

"Alejandro and Rosaura miss you," I say, suddenly desperate. It never occurred to me that my mission could be defeated by Isadora herself. "They'll be happy to welcome your child also."

Isadora laughs, but it's not the sweet laugh I remember. It's cold and sad and more than a little angry. It's cut off abruptly by a grimace.

"Is the child coming?" Miria asks.

"The contractions are minutes apart now. I managed to keep them from Papá when he visited. I have to get rid of this thing before it falls into the hands of that monster."

It takes every drop of will to stay focused on my task. "She can't ride through the night. We need another plan."

"We need a midwife," Miria says. "Maybe even a doctor."

"I'll lower you over the wall," I say. "Go with Lucio and Fernando to Brisadulce, tell the king what has happened. Tell him we have proof that Solvaño committed treason by intercepting a royal communication. Alejandro should send the Guard to arrest Solvaño. And Isadora and I might need rescuing if we are caught. It has to be you. You're the only one he knows and will believe."

"What will you do?"

I look at Isadora. "We'll hide in the city, maybe a tavern down by the docks." I'm making this up as fast as I can. "We'll stay out of sight until your return."

"That's a terrible plan," Miria says. "Too many things can go wrong."

"Do you have anything better?"

"No," she admits. "Here, take my cloak," she says to the shivering Isadora. "This will attract less attention down on the docks. If we could do something about the smell . . . You'll have to take everything off and just wear the cloak."

Isadora hesitates.

"Give us some privacy," Miria says.

I step out into the storeroom, then peer into the tower well for guards, knowing that each moment we delay increases our risk. But it remains empty for now.

The women emerge from Isadora's cell. Miria looks both ashen and furious. Isadora has kept her face wrapped—a wise choice, for we don't want anyone recognizing her.

We leave the storeroom and spiral down the stairs. From the tower, we sneak through the back hall to a door leading to the ramparts. This is the most tenuous part of our journey; if any guards ignored their bribes, they will be patrolling here.

We creep along, hunched over so that our figures are partly obscured by crenellations. I support Isadora as best I can. She stops occasionally, her hand becoming a vise on my arm as a contraction takes her.

At last we reach the southern wall. "Hurry!" Miria whispers.

I pull the rope from beneath my cloak and make two loops—a large one to wrap around my waist and slide the rope through, and a small one for Miria to stand in. Miria slips her foot into the loop, and I brace myself to lower her.

"When the time comes, just let things run their natural course," Miria tells me. "And be kind. She's been through a lot."

"I will treat her as if she is my next queen," I say.

"Wait!" Isadora says. "I need a weapon."

Miria takes a dagger from her belt and offers it, handle first. "May God watch over you both," she says. Isadora grabs the knife, and I let Miria's rope slide through my fingers.

My shoulders burn with the effort. We're taking too long. But suddenly the burden eases. Fernando and Lucio have steadied her from below. Then come two quick tugs on the rope—my signal to let go.

I toss the rope over the side of the wall. Hushed voices drift up, and then the sound of hooves, which gradually fade away.

"The only way out is through the front door," I say. There might be a little time left before the guards resume their patrols, but we'll have to be fast. "Ready?"

Her fingers close tight about my wrist, and she pants into another contraction. "Just get me out of here," she says breathlessly.

The bribes work. The way is clear, and we make it into the servants' wing, down the back stairs, and into the main hall. Our exit looms large when a door slams behind us. I whirl. Lord Solvaño bears down on us.

I throw my cloak around Isadora and pull her head to my chest. I keep my body angled to block his view. My heart pounds and my palms sweat as I quickly consider my options, which range from knocking him down and running out with Isadora in my arms to simply running. . . .

"I was just coming to find you, Squire Hect— What's the meaning of this?" he says. "Who do you have there?"

Isadora giggles, a sound that comes across as half mad, and reaches around my side to squeeze my rear.

"You've brought a lady of the docks into my home?" he says. Surely, he is not that stupid. Surely, he has heard reports by now of our scouting of the tower. Then I notice that he sways unsteadily, and his eyes shift as if struggling to find focus.

"I assure you no money has been exchanged," I say, because I'm not sure what else to say. Isadora has another contraction, and her suggestive hand turns into a hard squeeze that makes my eyes water. I brace us to keep us both from collapsing. She presses her face against my chest and fights for control, but still looses a choked-off grunt that makes my heart ache for her.

Her father's face turns red. "If you weren't the king's envoy, I'd beat you both out into the street this instant." He gesticulates wildly as he says it, which throws him off balance, and he staggers.

Isadora's contraction eases, as does her grip. She straightens, looks me in the eye, breathes deep. Though her eyes are rimmed with red and sunken, they are still beautiful. "We were just leaving," I say gently to her. I back us both away, keeping myself between him and his daughter. Thank God he is drunk.

"You both should be stripped and lashed and . . . God, what is that smell? Even a lady of the docks should have *some* pride."

Isadora plants herself, stopping us.

"What are you—?"

She rips away from my grasp. Before I can stop her, before I can even breathe, she whips Miria's dagger out from beneath her cloak and bears down on her father.

"Isadora!" Solvaño gasps. "You *whore*. I should have—"

I reach for her, but she is lightning fury. "How dare you!" she cries. "I did everything you asked. Your ambition made me this way. *You* did this." She gestures emphatically with the dagger; its blade winks in the torchlight. "And you dare call *me* a whore?"

"Isadora, let's go," I plead. "Your father has committed treason. He'll pay for what he has done. But we need to get away."

"You were supposed to become queen," Solvaño says. Spittle edges his mouth now as he steps forward, seemingly unaware of Isadora's dagger. "How you failed so utterly, I'll never—"

"He picked her because of you! He couldn't bear the idea of you as a father-in-law." The hand holding the dagger wavers, then drops to her side. "I couldn't blame him, even when he broke my heart."

His grin is smug. "You're a whore *and* a liar. And now no one will want you. I've made sure of that."

A cry of anguish bubbles up from somewhere deep inside her as she raises the knife and plunges it into her father's belly.

"Isadora!" Oh, God, what has she done?

She yanks out the knife. Blood bubbles up from the wound as she raises it again, but I grab her elbow. "Let's go, my lady. Before the alarm goes up."

She drops the dagger. It clatters to the stone floor, and droplets of blood sprinkle around it.

Solvaño makes a gurgling noise as he raises his head. He's trying to say something. His face shows no surprise, no fear of dying. There is only hate.

"How could he," Isadora whispers. "His own daughter."

"He was a monster," I agree, staring at the body twitching on the floor.

"I guess I've had my revenge," she whispers, but she doesn't sound convinced.

"Yes. Now let's go. No, wait."

I crouch beside Solvaño's body, thinking. Then I grab the dagger, and bile rises in my throat as I place the tip against the still-seeping wound and send the dagger home.

"What—what are you doing?" Isadora says.

I wrap Solvaño's right hand around the knife grip, then with a grunt and heave, I roll him over onto his stomach. "I'm trying to make it look like an accident," I explain. I stand and look down at my handiwork, feeling sick. "The king's advisers can manufacture whatever story they want of this, but it will help if your father's people find the body this way."

Isadora laughs again, her laugh dissolving into tears. She stumbles as another spasm takes her, and I rush to her side. We are both sticky with blood as I prop her up to pant through the contraction. I breathe along with her, trying to still my own heart. I'm in deep waters, way over my head. I have no idea what to do next, except to keep moving, so that's what we do—out the front door, through the gardens and the rusty gate, and down the road toward the docks.

We have just reached the closed-up market stalls when Isadora's knees buckle. "This is it," she gasps between breaths. "I can't go on."

I panic, turning in a circle, but I don't even know what I'm looking for. Why did I send Miria away for help?

Isadora grips my hand, her tiny fingers squeezing so hard, I think she will break my bones. They are slick with her father's blood. "Just get me to someplace where I can lie down," she gasps again.

I use the handle of my dagger to break the latch on one of the stall doors, and I help her inside.

The ground is hard-packed, with pebbles here and there. At least it's out of the wind and ocean spray. I pull the queen's quilt from my pack. I fold it in half once, then spread it out and support Isadora as she lowers herself gingerly on top of it.

Her labored breaths suck at the linen wrapping her face. "Here, let me help you," I say, reaching for her face.

But she screams at me. "No!"

The contractions are coming fast and hard now, and I have no idea what to tell her, but she seems to know what to do, so I sit and hold her hand and say over and over that things will be all right.

She continues to have trouble breathing through the cloth. Finally, she yells, "Don't look at me, do *not* look at me," and she pulls it away from her face.

Of course, I look, but I don't believe what I see.

Her nose has been sliced off her face, leaving two gaping nostril holes, like those of a skull. Her cheeks have been slashed with a knife and are covered with red, raw scars, where they are still healing.

Solvaño intended to make a monster of Isadora, and maybe, in inciting her killing rage, he did.

I've never wanted to murder anyone. Most men go through their whole lives without having to kill, and there is no glamor in it for me. But in this moment, if Lord Solvaño were here, I would kill him all over again.

Isadora is trapped between sobbing and pushing. The baby is eager to be born.

"It is going to be all right," I tell her. "Everything is going to be all right."

"Stop lying to me!" she screams.

So I sit and hold her hand and wipe the sweat from her forehead and from her still-healing scars, and I tell her about her cousin the queen, who made this quilt that she's lying on, and how the commander of the Guard called me a princess for having it. I try to project calm, although I feel anything but calm.

"Oh, God, here it comes," she cries.

"What do I do?"

"Get it out of me!"

I freeze. I've never . . . We need another woman here. Maybe I should go find someone. . . .

"GET IT OUT."

I'm trembling as I lift the cloak and reveal her naked body. "Oh, God." She is like a two-headed monster, with that wet, grayish-blue head poking out from between her legs. I reach for it with shaking hands, then cradle it in my palm and help support it as she pushes again. The whole thing slips out in a wave of blood-tinged wetness.

I've never seen anything born before, not even a colt or a kitten. Just this squirming boy, his mouth open in a silent scream. He hardly looks like a person, all pale and glinting wet in our meager light. I lift him up, offer him to her, but she shakes her head.

"No, I don't want it, it's not mine, I don't." She is limp on her back now, spent, her gaze shifted away.

"What should I do?" I say. Just then, the baby shudders, and a great wail fills the empty market stall.

"Leave it to die."

"No!" I say. "What do I do with the cord?" Determination settles into my core, giving me strength and new energy. If his mother doesn't want him, that leaves me with only one course.

Because I know whose child this is. And Alejandro will want his son. I must deliver this royal bastard to his father. It's the right thing to do.

"Still have your knife?" she asks.

"Yes."

"Then tie a knot and cut the cord above the knot."

"You'll have to hold him while I do it," I say.

She looks angry, but she holds out her arms, and I hand her the child. The cord is warm and slick in my fingers and slips when I try to cut it, but I soon have the job done.

"Can you wipe him off?" she says. He is rooting around, trying to get his face at her breasts.

"Of course," I say. I half cut, half rip two strips from the quilt where it is still mostly clean. We use one piece to wipe him off and the other to wrap him up. By the time that's done, the baby is feeding, and Isadora is crying, tears running down the furrows between the scars on her cheek.

"You were marvelous," I tell her, and I mean it. "Getting out of the tower, delivering the baby." Killing her father.

She shakes her head.

"I didn't know what to do," I press. "Not when we ran into your father, not when the baby was coming, but you made the right decisions every step of the way. You're a warrior."

She continues to shake her head. "What does it matter? I've nowhere to go."

"Yes, you do." I know exactly where to take her.

13

MY brother's ship, the *Aracely*—named after his wife—is the most beautiful ship in Joya d'Arena. It's a tiny *caravela* with three masts and a small crew, but a deep hold for cargo. Its lovely lines are trimmed in mahogany, which the crew keeps burnished through tide and storm. The doors and rail are painted the deep red of sacrament roses.

Though it is still deepest night, the crewman on watch recognizes me when I come aboard. He raises an eyebrow at the sight of a woman and baby, but says nothing. I help Isadora to the captain's quarters and beat on the door.

Felix yanks it open. He is shirtless, wild hair awry, but instantly alert. "Hector? What are you doing here?"

At that moment the baby cries, and Aracely appears at his shoulder.

Relief floods me. "We need help," I say.

Lantern light glints against glass beads in Felix's beard as he starts to speak, but Aracely shoves him out of the cabin. "Get out," she says to her husband. "Get us something to eat and drink but knock before you enter. And you," she says to Isadora and me, "inside now."

She pulls us through the door and closes it behind us. Sumptuous rugs cover the wooden plank floors. A desk sits in one corner, bolted down, and a large bed is built into the other. It is unmade, and the silk coverlet hangs over the edge and drags on the floor. Lanterns hang from the ceiling. They sway with the ship's gentle rocking, and shadows leap along the wood panel walls.

Aracely is a tall, large-boned woman with a strong chin and rich brown eyes like the mahogany of the ship that is named for her. She dwarfs Isadora as she leads her to the bed and helps her lie back. My sister-in-law is impervious to blood and stink as she pulls up the fine silk coverlet and tucks it around Isadora's shoulders. "What's your name, dear?"

"Isadora."

"That baby's less than an hour old, or I've never midwifed a child." She pulls down the swaddling with a forefinger to get a better look at him. "Some women can be up and walking right after, but you were already in bad shape, yes? Has the afterbirth passed?"

"Yes," Isadora says, somewhat stunned.

"Well, that's one thing done right," she says, and gives me a withering glance.

"I—"

"Hector de Ventierra." She's working up to a full sail of anger, which is not something I want aimed at my horizon. "You foolish, stupid boy, what in seven hells have you done to this poor—"

She stops because she has unwrapped Isadora's face. The girl's tears have dried up. Maybe she doesn't have any more, but she stares back at Aracely, one woman to another, with nothing to hide.

"Who did this?" Aracely says. Her voice is soft, but it snaps like a sail catching the wind, and I realize that I have never seen her so angry.

"My father," Isadora says.

"Lord Solvaño de Flurendi," I add. "Keeper of the Fortress of Wind and portmaster of Puerto Verde."

"I know who he is," Aracely says.

"He is on his way to the seven hells himself," I say. "I expect the cry to go up any moment."

Isadora turns her face away, guilty tears pooling in her eyes. For some reason, I'm a little relieved to see them.

Aracely swears in a language I don't understand, and then she goes to the door and yanks it open. Felix stands there with a tray of bread and cheeses and a jug of wine.

Aracely takes them from his hands and says, "We're leaving port at once. Cast off and get us out to sea, quietly as you can."

"Our cargo is only half sold, so . . ." He pauses, eyes narrowed, then says, "Setting sail for where, my dear?"

"Brisadulce," I answer.

He nods but stares at me hard. "We're going to have a talk, you and I."

"Not until I'm done with him," Aracely says, and she kicks

the door shut and latches it. She turns back to me. "So, this is not your child, after all."

I hope she doesn't notice my rising blush. "No."

She looks at both of us. "Can you say whose it is?"

"No," I say, before Isadora can answer.

Aracely looks at both of us, at the baby, and then back to my clothes, which are soaked in blood.

The ship rocks as it pushes away from the dock. I'm thrown off balance and stumble, but Aracely shifts her weight and keeps her feet. Outside, oars dip and splash as the pilot boat tows us toward the harbor mouth.

"Do you have a plan?" she asks.

"Yes, I'm going to take both of them to King Alejandro."

"No!" Isadora says, her voice panicked. "I can't return to court, not like this. I have no desire to see . . . him."

I open my mouth to argue, but Aracely says, "You don't have to do anything you don't want to do, and if this one, or anyone else, tries to make you, they'll have to go through me first."

Isadora grabs Aracely's hand. "You mean that?"

"I surely do. You'll have to do something. But it won't be what any man decides." She glances at me. "Not even if he is well-meaning."

I don't know if Aracely is referring to me or Alejandro—for she has surely guessed whose child this is—but it doesn't matter because I'm so relieved to let her take charge.

"But what can I do?" Isadora asks.

"Are you educated? Can you read and write and do figures? Are you willing to learn?"

"Yes. . . ."

"Then you have a thousand options. In the temperate mountains around Basajuan, you could farm a small plot of land and grow grapes or dates for winemaking. You could run a tavern in the free villages east of the desert. In the southern isles beyond Selvarica, women keep their faces covered all the time. You could set up as a merchant there and manage trade for us and for other ships."

"That—" Isadora says.

"Shh, you don't have to decide now."

"Where will I get the money?"

"You don't have to decide that now, either. But we'll find a way." The baby stirs from its sleep and roots around her chest again. "Perhaps from the baby's father."

"I won't ask for favors."

"It's not a favor he owes you." She pauses. "What do *you* want to do with the baby?"

Isadora hesitates, gazing down at the baby, a softness in her eyes that wasn't there before. Then her lips press into a firm line. "That's Hector's problem," she says finally, tilting her head at me. "I didn't want the child, and he chose to save him."

The cabin suddenly feels very small and crowded. At least she's calling him a child now.

"Well, that brings me back to where I intended to start with you," Aracely says, turning to me. "You are too young to act the father and raise this boy."

"Not me," I say. "But if you get me to Brisadulce, I know someone who wants him."

14

THE wind is poor, and it takes us four days to reach the capital. We set anchor, and Isadora gives the baby a final kiss on the forehead, then turns away, refusing to look again.

Aracely gives the baby two drops of duerma leaf tea, which she says will make him sleep. He is so tiny, especially swaddled tight in one of Aracely's blankets and wrapped in a sling under my cloak. I'll be able to smuggle him into the palace with no one the wiser.

"He'll need a nursemaid when he wakes," she says.

"What about Isadora? She could—"

"Leave her out of it. You promised you would take care of the child. Keep that promise. Felix and I will take care of her." She sighs, her eyes softening. "What will you do now— try to get back into the Guard?"

"Yes," I say, although it feels different now. And if I get another shot at it, I definitely want Fernando and Lucio with me.

"If it doesn't work out, we'll find something for you.

Isadora might need a business partner. If you use the stake I gave you—"

She reads something in my expression and stops, surprised.

"I needed it," I protest.

She nods. "Well, whatever you get now, you'll have to earn on your own. Good luck, Hector." She gives me a good-bye kiss on the cheek.

Felix stands by the gangplank. "We need to talk about this," he says. "I'm going to take a huge loss on my remaining cargo, now that it's so late."

"One day," I promise. "And thank you." I hope he's not too angry or disappointed with me.

But he gives me a single slight nod, and I know everything is all right between us.

I walk to the palace unaccosted. The guards at the portcullis—General Luz-Manuel's men—wave me through without question, but I feel their eyes on my back as I pass. I hope they are not noticing that it is far too warm for the cloak I wear.

If the Royal Guard at the inner gate are surprised to see me, they don't let on. Vicenç's eyes widen when I reach his desk, but he gestures for the pages to remain where they are and motions me through the reception area alone.

My footsteps do not falter until I reach Queen Rosaura's chamber. The baby stirs beneath my robes. Sweat forms on my forehead. I hope I've made the right decision.

A shape moves ahead of me. Alejandro paces in the hall.

"Your Majesty," I say.

He looks up, startled. Dark circles shadow his eyes, and lines of worry age his face. He rushes forward as if to embrace me. "Hector, I'm so glad you— What's that?" He pulls up short as I reach under my cloak for the baby.

"We should speak privately, sire," I say, revealing the now-wriggling bundle.

The door to the queen's chambers opens, and Dr. Enzo sticks his head out. "The queen requests your attendance, Your Majesty." He sees me. Then the baby. "Oh. You'd better come too."

We step inside. Rosaura is propped up near her balcony. Her face is pale and drawn. Her hair is plastered to her head with sweat, and her cheeks are wet with tears. I have seen too many tears in recent days.

Miria stands at her bedside. She still wears her traveling dress, stained with dirt and torn; she has also just arrived.

"Where's Isadora?" she says when she sees me.

I shake my head. "She refuses to come."

Rosaura reaches out her hands. "Is this her baby? Let me see."

Miria must have told her everything. I hand over the boy. He starts to twitch and fuss as soon as he leaves the warmth of my chest. He's wrapped in remnants of the queen's quilt, which is freshly laundered but faded from Aracely's attempts to remove the birthing stains. "I'm sorry, Your Majesty, but—"

Rosaura isn't listening. Her entire attention is captured by the baby. She takes him and cradles him gently to her chest. So different from Isadora. As if he is a precious gift.

She strokes the swirling dark hair on his head and whispers to him, and then she tucks him under her sweat-soaked shirt and takes him to her breast.

And suddenly I notice the other details—her flaccid belly, the bloody sheets wadded up in a corner, Dr. Enzo's sleeves rolled up.

Dr. Enzo catches my eye and shakes his head.

I look again and see that her cheeks are not just flushed with tears, but with fever. Something has gone terribly wrong, something even beyond the tragedy of losing her baby.

Alejandro drapes an arm across my shoulders. His gesture is casual, but his breath is jagged, and I get the feeling he's taking what comfort he can.

"How much has Miria told you?" I ask.

"Not much," Alejandro says.

"Everything," Rosaura answers. She presses her lips to the baby's head as he nurses. "I'm just so glad you're all back safely."

But we almost didn't make it back. Reluctantly, I say, "I know it's a bad time, but there are some things I have to tell you. You have to know . . ."

"Spit it out, Hector," Alejandro says.

"An assassin came after us. Only Lord-Commander Enrico and Captain Mandrano knew where we were going."

The room grows very still.

Alejandro steps away from me. He rubs at his chin, thinking hard. "I believe Captain Mandrano is above reproach in this instance."

"I agree." I take a deep breath. I'm about to lay accusations against a superior officer. "I know Enrico is personally ambitious and likes to consider himself a political player. Mandrano is the perfect second-in-command for him precisely because he hates politics and does not have ambition."

Everyone is staring at me sharply, but I press on.

"I don't know for sure that Enrico sent a killer after us. I can't prove it. I do know that during our short time in the training yard, I observed Mandrano's unquestioned loyalty to you, while Enrico did everything he could to subvert your commands."

"Such as?" Alejandro prods.

"In your letter, did you specify that Enrico was to send Tomás and Marlo with me?"

"Of course. Just like you asked."

"He sent two others instead—boys he thought were expendable, that the Guard would be well rid of."

Alejandro frowns. "We'll have to decide what to do about him."

He says it as if the decision is a nebulous, future thing. So very like my friend.

"Or you could decide now," Rosaura says gently.

"Give him what he wants," I press.

"Reward him?"

"Give him a title and a small estate somewhere remote. Mandrano is loyal and would mirror your votes in the Quorum for the next few years while you groomed another commander."

"And who should that be, do you think?" Alejandro asks.

"I have no idea! You're the king. *You* figure something out. Though this, at least, isn't a decision you must make right away."

Alejandro turns away and faces the wall, crossing his arms. Softly, he says, "We received word of Lord Solvaño's death just this morning. They delivered the weapon that killed him to me. It was a bronze dagger with a bone handle. The kind issued to attendants of the queen."

"I didn't—" Miria starts to protest, but I interrupt.

"That's the other thing I needed to tell you. I killed him."

Alejandro whirls to face me, and I step back involuntarily. But he's smiling. "Liar," he chides. "You're protecting her."

I wilt a little in relief.

"I admit, I was stunned," he says. "But it's actually not such a bad situation."

"I . . . I tried to make it look like an accident."

"Hector!" Rosaura exclaims.

But Alejandro is nodding. "Vicenç can start circulating the story. Rosaura's father will take over as portmaster. And now"—he brightens visibly—"Enrico can take custody of the Fortress of Wind."

"The place is in terrible disrepair," I say meaningfully. "And the staff there has been horribly abused. Everyone there will be glad for new leadership."

I recognize the mischievous glint in his eye. It used to indicate that he was about to send me to the kitchens to steal pollo pibil. "The fortress is a place of profound historical and architectural value," he says. "It should be painstakingly restored to its former glory."

"Such an important task could only be imparted to someone you trust implicitly."

"Like the retired commander of my Guard."

"We must find Isadora and do something to help her," Rosaura interjects.

"Oh, we will," Alejandro says, and I know by his inflection that the "we" is both personal and royal.

Rosaura grimaces as she tries to lift the baby.

"Here, let me burp him for you," Miria says, reaching for the child. She lays him across her shoulder and pats his back.

How do women all know what to do with babies? It's like they have their own special kind of sorcery.

"Who knows the whole story?" Alejandro asks. "About Isadora, the baby, her escape, your return."

"Only the people in this room. And Isadora. My brother and his wife know of her pregnancy and have probably made some guesses, but you can trust them. Some of Solvaño's servants knew Isadora was being held captive, but they weren't allowed to see her. Even Lucio and Fernando, the boys who went with me, know very little."

Dr. Enzo takes the child from Miria's arms. "Let me examine him," he says. Rosaura looks on longingly, as if she can't wait to have the baby back in her own arms.

"And how is Isadora?" Alejandro asks. "Is she still as beautiful . . ." He gives his wife an apologetic glance.

"She is everything you remember and more," I say firmly.

Alejandro smiles, an expression tinged with both joy and regret.

"Your Majesty, a word," Dr. Enzo says. He cradles the baby in his arms, even as he swipes a finger into the gumless mouth.

Alejandro steps over to the corner to talk to him in hushed tones.

"Hector," the queen calls, and I move to her side. She whispers, "Miria told me *everything* about Isadora. Thank you for your kindness to my husband. And thank you"—tears fill her eyes as she stares after the baby in Enzo's arms—"for him. You have given me an incredible gift, Hector."

There are so many things I want to say. *Your husband— my friend—does not deserve you,* being high on the list. I settle for, "You're welcome."

She smiles. "You're learning," she says. "The less you say, the more your words will matter."

"What now?" I ask.

"For you, I don't know," she says. "A young man who wantonly destroys a quilt handmade for him by the queen of the realm is unlikely to have a promising future."

Before I can reply, Alejandro turns and says, "The queen and I need some privacy. I probably don't have to tell you to speak to no one—but I am telling you, speak to no one."

I cast a final glance toward Rosaura, whose breathing has become weak and shallow. A rock of dread has settled in my gut, and I'm feeling miserable as we leave. I hold the door open for Miria.

"Thank you," I say to her. "For everything you did."

"Oh, I don't know if you want to thank me yet," she says.

"What does that mean?"

But she walks away without an explanation.

15

THE palace is frantically busy for the next few days while I sit in my old quarters, no longer the king's squire and not really a recruit for the Royal Guard. Vicenç ushers a stream of visitors in and out of the king's chambers, but I am not one of them.

Finally, we are called to the courtyard, every member of the palace household. We stand shoulder to shoulder, all mixed together: Royal Guard and palace watch, laundresses and stable boys, the queen's ladies and even a few in-residence nobles.

Lucio and Fernando find me in the crowd. It's the first time I've seen them since returning from Puerto Verde.

"Did you hear about the lord-commander?" Lucio whispers.

"No," I say. I haven't heard anything.

"He resigned from the Guard. You heard that Solvaño got roaring drunk and fell on his dagger, right? Well, the king has assigned Enrico guardianship of the Fortress of Wind."

Fernando is eager to confirm this. "Rumor is the resignation was *forced*. He's to leave at once to tend to the restoration of the tower."

"How nice for him," I say. "He must be happy to finally be a lord of his own land."

"It's awful," Lucio says. "Mandrano's been named interim lord-commander. He made us scrub the training yard."

I grin. "But on the positive side, he dumped your wine."

This earns me a staggering cuff on the shoulder, but Lucio is grinning too.

I search for Mandrano and find him standing near the front. Beside him is Miria. They are holding hands.

Of course.

I immediately regret every word I've ever said about him.

He catches me looking at him and glowers. So much for my hope of returning to the Guard. Rosaura's warnings to keep my mouth shut were meant in more ways than I could have ever guessed.

Alejandro and Rosaura appear at the balcony above us. The buzz of conversation in the courtyard falls silent. They wear royal white, and their golden crowns shimmer in the sunshine. Rosaura's face is as pale as death, and I know, because I know her, that it is taking all her strength and focus to be here. Even so, she manages to exude radiant purpose.

Dr. Enzo approaches from behind, carrying a small bundle in his arms.

Alejandro takes the baby from him and holds him up for the crowd.

Alejandro's voice booms, "Her Majesty Queen Rosaura and I announce the birth of our son and heir to the throne. Please welcome your future king, Prince Rosario né Flurendi de Vega!"

The crowd goes wild. The baby jerks in Alejandro's arms and starts to squall, which sends everyone into an even louder frenzy of cheering.

Rosario.

Poor boy. He had such a rough beginning. But with Alejandro for a father and Rosaura for his mother, life ought to get a lot better for him. At least I hope so.

Lucio and Fernando cheer with everyone else. "I guess we missed all the important stuff while we were away in Puerto Verde," Lucio says to me. "What happened with Lady Isadora? Miria said you got her away safely."

"Yes. Everything turned out well for her," I say.

"Good. Though it was probably all for nothing, since her father ended up killing himself anyway."

"Yes," I say. "All for nothing."

16

So here we stand, nine recruits in the training yard of the palace. Lucio and Fernando stand beside me.

The morning sun beats down on our scalps as Interim Lord-Commander Mandrano enters the yard.

"Lord-Commander Enrico has been given a new assignment," he says. "So I've been instructed to start the recruiting season over from scratch. I will oversee your training until the king appoints a new lord-commander."

I'm sure Miria has something to do with how everything has played out, but if I were a gambling man, I'd lay odds that Miria and I will never speak of it.

"The only thing a recruit gets for free is the opportunity to prove himself," Mandrano continues. "Anything you get after that, you earn. Are you ready to *earn* the title of Royal Guard?"

"Yes, my lord!" we shout in unison.

Mandrano twitches at the word "lord," but he doesn't protest. He walks down the line, asking the recruits about the items they've brought with them. When he comes to me, he discovers that my hands are empty.

"Did you bring three personal items, recruit?" he asks.

"Yes, my lord!" I say.

"What are they?"

"Love for my kingdom, love for my king, and love for my queen, my lord!"

He pauses for a long time before he nods. "I can work with that," he says finally.

It's all a Royal Guard, a *true* Royal Guard, will ever need.